Room to Breathe

Also by JoAnn Bren Guernsey

Journey to Almost There
Five Summers

Room to Breathe

JoANN BREN GUERNSEY

Clarion Books

TICKNOR & FIELDS: A HOUGHTON MIFFLIN COMPANY

New York

Clarion Books
Ticknor & Fields, a Houghton Mifflin Company
Copyright © 1986 by JoAnn Bren Guernsey
Printed in the U.S.A.
Library of Congress Cataloging-in-Publication Data
Guernsey, JoAnn Bren.
Room to breathe.
Summary: Seventeen-year-old Mandy often plays the
helpless role with her father and boyfriend, but as she
becomes caught up in the social turmoil of the late 1960s,
she begins to feel the need to assert her
independence.
[1. Self-assertion—Fiction] I. Title.
PZ7.G9357Ro 1986   [Fic]   86-2688
ISBN 0-89919-465-6

s 10 9 8 7 6 5 4 3 2 1

For K. L. W.

Memories sifted become finer.

I

THERE WAS SOMETHING very familiar about the whole scene, and yet I could not for the life of me remember ever being on a picnic with Peter and my father. Just the three of us — cozy and complete, or trying to be. No scene could ever be complete again, I knew. Mom had left behind an enormous space; we had been walking around it the entire three months since her death.

"Nothing like a Labor Day picnic," Peter said, "to close the summer. Last picnic of the season. For that matter, the last picnic of 1969, of the decade."

"Peter," I reminded him, "we didn't go on any other picnics this summer."

He moved over to me from where he had been re-packing our things into the old, frayed basket. The wicker was soft with use — Mom's old basket, her mom's before that. Peter's spare, strong arms enveloped me as if to say he knew I was thinking about my mother and missing her arms. "Details, details. First picnic, last picnic. It's momentous anyway."

It had been over two years since Peter had happened across our farm for a summer job. And, with the exception of a few months that he had gone to school in New York, we had been together much of that time.

Dad stood up stiffly, shook his long limbs and stretched. A lifetime of farmwork had made him ruggedly muscular. The only thing soft about him were his pale blue eyes. He tried on a grin, but it didn't fit. "That was delicious, Mandy. What a great little cook you've turned out to be."

"Not me. It was —"

"Isn't she, though? A great cook." Peter gave me a meaningful look. "Like her mom."

At first his words seemed designed to squeeze me tighter than his arms, and I wanted to pull away. Why, I wondered, was Peter insisting on this pretense that I had put the picnic together when it was all his doing? But then I was grateful to him for mentioning Mom, even if it was to compare me to her; so few people were willing to talk about her in front of me or Dad.

"I have it all figured out," Peter continued. "How you'll be cooking for me every now and then, since I'll be moving off-campus this year."

"I will?" So that's what he was up to. I made a move to finish packing.

He dropped his arms away from me and gestured innocently with them. "Hey, you know what I mean. You'll be helping *me* learn to cook for myself, right?"

"Sure. I guess I can do that." Even though it was 80°, I felt a chill after Peter and I had withdrawn from each other. I automatically wanted his arms back around me, where they seemed to belong.

Dad glanced at Peter, then at me, and back to Peter. "Wait a minute. You're getting an apartment?"

"Sure thing," Peter answered. "Any day now. I haven't quite found the right . . . oh, I don't know, atmosphere . . . yet." He gave me a sly smile that quickened my pulse. His ability to melt away any resentment I might have felt with something as simple as a smile or a touch amazed me. Sometimes it frightened me as well.

"You'll probably have a roommate," Dad said.

Peter paused. "Well, yes. I guess Gretchen will be moving in with me."

"Gretchen?" Dad was getting more flustered by the minute.

"You know about my *other* girl, don't you, George?"

Dad opened his mouth, then closed it again.

Peter continued, "My dad says it's okay with him — although he would just as soon have kept her for himself."

Dad's color was becoming alarming. His pale eyes blinked at me and I figured it was time he was rescued.

"Dad, Gretchen is just Peter's old cat. Honestly, Peter. You're incorrigible."

Peter accepted what he considered my praise with a good-natured shrug and finished packing. The red-and-white checked tablecloth, clumsily folded, fit in last, on top. Where, I wondered, had he found that? His determination to make everything look as it should, down to the checked tablecloth, touched me now instead of

3

bothering me, and I brushed up against him when he reached for a stray napkin.

Dad had recovered and seemed cheerier again, but his eyes followed my movement. There was a new puppyish quality about them lately that made me sad and sorry for him. It also made me flinch; his eyes kept reaching for me, as if I could somehow fill the emptiness they expressed.

"So," Dad said. "What are you two doing tonight? Once you get rid of me, that is."

I started to protest until I noticed that he was looking at Peter, asking him exclusively. This had become his way during the summer. He would practically say, "Hey, Peter, how's our little Mandy feeling today?"

Peter closed the trunk of his ancient blue Chevy, and the remains of our picnic abruptly disappeared. "Well, I'm not sure. I thought we'd try to find a band playing somewhere."

"How about a movie?" I asked.

"Another movie? I swear we've seen everything there is to see around here. Maybe twice."

I frowned at him. "We have not."

"It sure seems like —"

"Oh, never mind. We'll do whatever you want." I knew Peter found going to movies our least intimate kind of date. The way I threw myself so totally into whatever story was unfolding before us on the huge, bright, inviting screen tended to put distance between Peter and me. His arm would tighten around me, he'd begin to nuzzle my neck and kiss me, but he always could tell I was slipping away from him and into that other, magnified dramatic embrace.

"Movie's fine." Peter spread his arms and smiled. "Whatever makes you happy makes me happy."

"No, that's okay."

Dad was watching, his head pivoting from one to the other of us.

"Tell you what," Peter said. "Why don't we go to a movie and you go with us, George. You haven't been to a movie in ages, have you?"

When I wondered, had Peter stopped calling my dad Mr. Smetana?

"Well," Dad said, "I suppose it has been a while. But —"

"It's settled, then. We'll all go." Peter flung his arms out and slapped them at his sides. He was acting so excited even I believed him, so I was sure Dad would too. "Let's go pick up a newspaper and decide what to see."

"There's this John Wayne picture I've been meaning to see," Dad mumbled, "but I don't want to get in the way of your fun."

But, as Peter had said, it was settled. Being three years older than me, and much appreciated by my dad right from the start, Peter was effective at taking charge.

I sat between them in the car and again in the theatre. On one side, Peter's arm remained politely touching mine on the armrest, while on the other, Dad's shoulder rose protectively above mine. If I tried to move either way, I would meet resistance.

Halfway through the movie, which for once I was

5

scarcely watching at all, I felt so completely and irreversibly trapped that I knew a powerful scream would rise from deep inside me if I didn't get out of that seat. What, I wondered, would happen then?

I clenched my jaws and mashed my lips tightly together against the scream that was banging at them from the inside. Not daring even to say "Excuse me," I pushed my way past Peter and what seemed hundreds of unyielding bodies beyond him. Thrust into the openness of the aisle at last, I fled up the incline, into the lit lobby and to the rest room.

"Mom," I said aloud, once safely inside and alone. "Mom." I couldn't seem to breathe. Pacing back and forth in front of the fluorescent-lit mirror, I gulped for air, swallowed down what was left of the scream. Maybe I should have let it come out. Maybe it would lie in wait for me later, when I least expected. I was afraid I would soon stop breathing altogether and then neither screaming nor anything else would be possible.

But then, finally, there she was. As always. Mom. I felt her presence so strongly, I looked into the mirror expecting to see her face — round, the way it had been before her long illness — smiling moonbeams at me. "Mom," I said, gasping. "What am I . . . going to . . . do?"

"Breathe" was her reply.

Staring alternately at my own blotchy, panicked face in the mirror and at the space next to it where Mom's face should be, my breathing began to return to normal.

Several minutes later, I found Peter waiting for me in

the lobby. His face, above the dark beard, was ashen and his black shaggy hair had the look of having been raked through repeatedly by his agitated fingers. "Are you okay?"

I let myself be folded into his concern. He warmed me, soothed me with his touch, and I cried.

"Hey, that's good," he said. "That's the way."

"No. I'm sorry."

"Sorry? Why? For crying? My God, Mandy, your mom died. She meant so much to you. Well, to us all, actually."

I eased one of my arms out of his firm grip.

"Your dad's devastated," Peter continued. "Sam and Greg live so far away now, they're not really like brothers anymore. You're feeling alone. I know."

"No, Peter, that's not exactly —"

"But, honey, you've got me. Always. I love you. Don't you see that?"

I freed my other arm and turned away from him slightly, wiping gingerly at my eyes. Black mascara striped the backs of my index fingers, and I stared at the marks as though they were a coded message.

"Doesn't it help? That I love you, I mean. Doesn't it?" He sounded worried now. His questions needed answers, and only I could give him the right ones.

What could I tell him? That what always helped me the most was talking to a ghost? That between him and Dad, I was suffocating? I tilted my face up toward his. "Yes, of course it helps. I love you, too, Peter."

There. That was it, his sustenance. And I hadn't really

lied. I did love him. It had to be possible to love Peter and breathe at the same time. I needed him at least as much as he needed me, didn't I?

He grinned and kissed me lightly, his lips moist and soft, tasting of popcorn salt. I wondered how mine felt and tasted to him. "Want to go back inside?" he asked.

"I guess we'd better. Dad will feel . . . deserted."

After the movie I still felt shaky and suggested we go home. But, of course, first came more food. My stomach sourly vetoed each item on the menu, but I forced half a sundae down anyway. Mom could never bear to see people not eat; I would eat to please her.

Dad and Peter chatted about the movie, a blustery John Wayne western. Dad shook his head admiringly about the steadfast cowboy and his daring deeds.

"I don't know," I said after having remained silent for what seemed like hours. "He's not my type at all."

Dad raised his eyebrows, and Peter hid a smile behind one hand.

"That super tough-guy act," I said. "It's just a way of making women feel small and helpless."

"Hey, wait just a dawg-gone minute." Peter straightened his sharply right-angled shoulders and swelled his chest as if to beat on it with his fists. "The Duke and I, we're one of a kind. So don't mess with me, woman."

In spite of myself, I giggled. "I'll try to keep that in mind."

Dad shook his head some more and then polished off the last of his banana split. "I suppose you can't finish," he said to me. For Peter's information, he added, "She eats like a bird."

I almost pointed out to him that, in fact, I had quite a hearty appetite, at least when I felt good. But to avoid questions about exactly why I was feeling so lousy, I pushed my dish toward Dad. Watching Dad eat, I realized that he had put on a few pounds, and I was glad. Although he hadn't exactly been thin for years — not since my much older brothers had been little — he had lost weight during Mom's last bout with cancer. The waiting and the pain seemed to melt something away from him, drop by drop.

"Are you both going back to school tomorrow?" Dad asked. He was getting that abandoned look again, the one that seemed to beg for reassurance that, no, I wouldn't be going to school after all. That my senior year was of no importance, nor was college after that.

"Just Mandy," Peter answered for us. "The U doesn't start up again 'til late September."

"Still in music, are you?" Dad seemed to want to postpone going home, asking questions to which he already knew the answers.

"I guess you could say that. I'm still playing as much as I can. I get some pretty good gigs, and teach kids and stuff like that." Peter looked embarrassed. "But after that fiasco last year at Juilliard . . ." I looked at him hopefully. Maybe at last he was going to talk about his leaving Juilliard after only one term. "Anyway," Peter said instead, "I guess teaching is about my best bet. It sure beats the hell out of going to 'Nam."

We all glanced at one another and then down at the sticky table. It was always hard to rescue a conversation after the mention of the war and the possibility of Peter or anyone else getting drafted. The boys in my class were already in the process of scurrying around figuring out what alternatives to the draft were open to them. Everybody seemed to have friends or relatives there. Many were not coming back.

I remembered, along with Dad, the long year we'd waited for my brother Sam to return from Vietnam. My other brother, Greg, had been luckier — or perhaps smarter; I was never sure what to call it. But what about Peter, I wondered. As long as he was in school, he figured he was safe. But he hated school now. It was worthless to someone who just wanted to play his trumpet.

I felt an unexpected urge to talk about all this — Peter's months away from us in New York, school, his goals, and for that matter, mine. It was appropriate that Dad be included. But the waitress brought our check, and Peter and Dad both stood up, suddenly restless.

"Oh, now we can go home?" I said. Now that I wanted to stay and talk.

Peter missed my sarcasm, perhaps deliberately. "Sure thing."

"Yes, it is a school night, after all," Dad added. "Mandy needs her beauty sleep."

I gave a little laugh, startling them both. Dad had never been one to utter such tired old fatherly remarks, and I couldn't help but laugh. It was either that or be more frightened by the change in him.

"I guess Mandy figures she's beautiful enough." Peter's voice had an edge to it. I wasn't sure if he was put off by my laughter or by my behavior in general. "Well," he said with a shrug, apparently determined not to let anything spoil his day, "she is, of course. Beautiful enough for me."

"Of course," Dad agreed.

I almost echoed, on cue, "Of course," but then I realized what I had to do instead.

When Peter slid into the driver's seat and Dad waited for me to take my place between them, I rounded the car to Peter's side and touched his shoulder. "How about if I drive us home tonight?"

Peter smiled. "No, I don't think so. You're pretty tired tonight."

"No, I'm not. I don't feel tired at all." I struggled to keep my voice sweet and soft. "I'm a very good driver, you've said so yourself, and I've got my purse with my license in it. Please."

Peter hesitated. It was difficult, I knew, for him to say no to me. But something else seemed to be working its way into his decision. Something strong and more difficult to deny than even my wishes. "Maybe next time, honey."

My touch on his shoulder turned heavier and sharp-fingered. "Peter, it's important to me."

Dad started to say something from over on his side of the car, but I interrupted him. "I really want to drive home tonight. I've driven your car before. What's the big deal?"

"Yeah, that's what I'd like to know," Peter said. "What *is* the big deal?"

Finally I let go of his shoulder and opened the rear door. "All right, then. If I'm so tired, I'll just get in back here and lay down my poor sleepy little head." I slammed the door closed and glared at Peter in the rearview mirror.

Dad slipped into the car and quietly closed his door, ushering in a soothing darkness. But I could see that they exchanged glances and, rather than have to look at them do that, I did, in fact, lie down. The vinyl seat was cold against my cheek and it smelled like feet. But anything was better than sitting between them again, all the way home.

2 ⟜

MY NEW CLOTHES were just outrageous enough.
They lay on my bed, arranged perfectly from
top to blue panty hose toes, as though I had been in
them, then evaporated. The boldly multicolored blouse
had puffy long sleeves that looked capable of gulping
and holding air, maybe even of levitation. The navy
blue miniskirt bordered on "micro," but a strange impulse earlier that August had made me buy it.

I would never have dared appear before Dad dressed
in such an outfit before, but now I felt a need to decide
for myself how to dress. Maybe the first day of my senior
year would mark the start of a new strategy.

After putting on my short skirt, I turned around slowly
in front of the mirror. Dropping something on the floor
could mean leaving it there rather than bending over in
front of some overly interested boy. But, experimenting
with a slight bend-over, I successfully resisted tugging
the stretchy fabric downward. Not bad. I had a good,
lean, strong-looking body. How could someone like me
be just someone's little girl?

I fluffed up my chin-length hair for the hundredth time, stuck my makeup kit into my purse and headed down the stairs. I could smell the pancakes Dad had prepared, and I knew I had to try to eat something. Dad's efforts in the kitchen could not go unappreciated, even though they were his way of saying, "You can do this much better, so next time you do it." Closing my eyes, I whispered, "Mom, if you can, please help me through this day."

"Morning, Dad." Sitting down quickly, I helped myself to juice and one of the cold doughy disks waiting for me. It was not quite burnt on one side, pale as cream on the other.

"Morning." Dad's voice reached me from behind his newspaper. "I'm afraid those pancakes are really awful. I wanted to let you sleep in."

"They look fine to me." I gobbled down a few bites to prove my point.

He lowered his paper just enough to stare at me over it.

I nearly blurted out that I'd get up earlier and make breakfast from now on, but instead I said, "I'm surprised you're not already out working."

He let the paper crumple into his lap and started rubbing his eyes with his fingertips. The skin of both his face and hands were dry and tough, and the rasping sound reminded me of my mom's pumice stone scrubbing away at her hands. "Farmer's hands," she had called them, sometimes with pride, more often with irritation.

"You're working way too hard, Dad," I said, "for this time of year, aren't you?"

He grunted from behind his fingers.

"I remember your saying that, compared with the work load all spring and summer, September was a snap. Things practically start harvesting themselves." I recalled the image that comment used to evoke from me: tomatoes, heads of cauliflower, and round, perfect pumpkins marching in from the fields in neat straight lines, maybe to Disneyish music.

"That's a lot of bull," Dad said, blinking at me now from rubbed-raw eyes. "There's a ton of work for me to do. Too much for one person, that's for sure."

"Well, I can't be here. What about Peter? He's been helping out now and then."

"Too busy this month, he says." Dad gave me a meaningful look. "Probably apartment hunting, and then moving in."

I figured Dad wanted reassurance from me that I would not be a participant in wild orgies anytime soon, but the fact was that the subject of Peter's apartment made me rather uneasy as well. It meant no more parking in dark lots, no more necking on our living-room couch, accompanied by Dad's snoring two rooms away. No more "kid stuff."

I decided to stick to the subject of farmwork. "Why don't you hire someone, then?"

"No."

"Why not?" I knew that it was because Mom had always taken care of hiring extra hands. She had, in fact, been the one who had hired Peter two summers ago.

Dad looked as though he was fighting the urge to rub

his eyes some more, dig at them, alleviate the itchiness of his entire body. "Maybe you're right. After school, let's talk about it. You can —"

"No. What do I know about this, anyway?" I didn't need to take on another of Mom's jobs, another chance to fall short. "The work has always been good for you. It keeps your mind busy and away from . . . other things. You can probably handle it."

I squeezed down some juice through the tightness in my throat and checked my watch. "Almost time for me to go."

Although I had not been expecting it, I certainly was not surprised when the familiar blue Chevy turned into our yard as I cleared away dishes. It gave a gritty blast of greeting and then sighed to a stop. I sighed back.

For a moment I toyed with the idea of sneaking out the back door and waiting on the road for my bus. But that would be crazy. "Dad, Peter's here," I said. I wished for once he'd say something like, "What, again?" The predictability I found sometimes irritating was, to Dad, a consolation.

"Hm-m-m? What is that you're wearing?"

I had stood up and forgotten about my miniskirt. Using my chair as a partial shield, I said, "This? Oh, I showed you this last month when I got it."

"You did? Isn't it awfully —"

"It's the style, Dad."

I made a big clatter stacking dishes and didn't hear Peter enter the house. He did not ring the doorbell, of course; he was at home with us.

Waiting for the sink to fill with water, I tried, unsuccessfully, to take deep breaths. Peter's eyes were pinned on me. His presence was somehow stifling to me, especially that morning of expected fresh beginnings. "Okay, okay," I said. "Go ahead and say what you're thinking." A frying pan slapped the dishwater and splashed it all over my new blouse. "Oh, fine. Great." I dabbed at it with a towel.

"You're not going to school dressed like *that*, are you?" Peter asked. "George, look at your crazy daughter. Are you going to allow her to expose her thighs to the whole school?"

"They're my thighs. And I wish you'd stop calling my dad George. It sounds disrespectful."

Dad was still trying to get a good look at me around the table and chair.

I sighed. "Peter, what are you doing here?" I gave up on the dishes. They would get done somehow. Later. "My bus will be here any minute. Excuse me."

He was blocking my way out of the kitchen. "I'm taking you to school today." He grinned at me and bowed with exaggerated chivalry.

Another sigh. I sensed that today would be a day full of sighs. It was an effective way of keeping myself breathing deeply. Today, I decided, it would be a waste of effort to try to talk Peter out of giving me a ride. But tomorrow, and the next day . . . all the days until his classes finally started again at the University? Would I have a chauffeur for four weeks? There must be some way to explain to him that it was suddenly important to me to get on that bus alone (cranky or confident or however I felt like being at the moment) and face the school day on my own. But he had already conveniently forgotten about our battle of wills last night. Somehow his "Sorry, honey" and sweet good-night kiss had solved everything for him.

"Peter . . ."

"Yes?" He picked up a couple of pancakes, examined them and then tried to juggle them for a moment before discreetly replacing them on the plate.

"I don't. . . that is, well, you must have better things to do with your mornings." I couldn't seem to control my nastiness. "I'm fully capable of getting to school on my own. Really. I've been doing it for years and not once have I gotten lost."

He turned to Dad. "Still the little ray of sunshine in the morning, isn't she?"

I tried again to push past him.

He shifted back and forth in front of me. "Come on now, Mandy. This is one of your jokes, dressing like that for me, isn't it? They probably don't even allow those skirts in school. And besides, you've got way too much eye makeup on. You look like a raccoon."

"I'm not dressing like this for *you*."

"Look, Mandy. I'm here to take you to school. I could have slept in, I could've eaten breakfast —"

Maybe he'd thought I would make it for him.

"— and I could have driven someone else to school, for that matter. But, fool that I am, I chose to do this nice thing for you. You hate the bus. I thought you'd be grateful."

18

I turned to kiss Dad's forehead. "Bye, Dad. I'll clean the kitchen when I get home. Thanks for breakfast. I'll take my turn tomorrow."

"I'm afraid we'll starve if you don't," Dad said.

His helplessness was hard for me to take, but I figured if there was anyone in the world I felt sorrier for than myself, it was him.

"We'll discuss that miniskirt when you get home today," Dad called to me after I'd left the kitchen.

I gathered together my notebooks and flute and headed toward my limo for the day. Peter followed at some distance and I felt his eyes fastened on me again. "Stop staring, will you?"

"If you didn't want to be stared at, you'd have worn something else. Those stupid skirts are passé anyway."

"Oh? Really? They're pah-say? My, that's interesting coming from a guy who wears threadbare jeans and plaid shirts every minute of the day. You look like you're still working on this farm. Where's your silly canvas hat? And your hoe?"

I hated the way I was behaving, and I couldn't quite look at him. I watched some dry leaves chasing each other in circles between our feet. But Peter simply opened the car door for me and bowed again, unflappable.

I tried to smile; I wanted so much to be happy, riding to school with this boy who loved me, really loved me. I wanted to sail through the day like a senior should, with cool, studied indifference. But I plopped into Peter's front seat crankier than ever.

"Hey," Peter said, "I'm sorry. I know how you hate it when I tell . . . uh, suggest how you should dress and stuff. You've got fabulous legs . . . might as well show them off, I suppose."

I looked at him. "Stop being so nice."

We were silent the whole way to school. My stomach growled, and I hugged my notebooks tighter against it. At a painfully quiet Stop sign, I heard Peter inhale and swallow a few times, as if preparing to say something, then changing his mind.

Finally he parked the car where the buses would soon be lining up, reached across me to open my door and said, "See you later."

The open door let in a rush of frigid, gas-smelly air. Maybe if I kiss him good-bye, I thought, everything will be all right. The sensation I often got from Peter's kisses of sinking into a warm bubble bath would be a welcome relief. But no. That would be too easy, too much of an escape. From what? I wondered. To what?

"Bye," I said as I slid out of the car and climbed the steps to my school. The car took off without an angry kick to the accelerator, but I figured I would be riding the bus tomorrow.

*

My friend Lynn was waiting at our adjoining lockers, as I thought she would be. She fidgeted with her purse strap as I approached, however, apparently uncertain whether or not to try to rush off before I reached her. I must have looked pretty glum.

Was this the first time I had seen Lynn since Mom's death? I wondered. No, she and her family had come to the funeral. But then they had spent the entire summer, as always, at their cabin. In a way, this was another of the precarious "firsts" I had been experiencing.

The summer had been full of them: the first trip to the grocery store (I had considered changing to one run by strangers), the first time passing Mom's favorite dress shop, the first encounters with her women friends, the first greeting from the mailman as he brought the pastel stack of condolence cards.

"Hi, Lynn."

She smiled shyly at me, still fidgeting. "Hi. How was your sum——— uh, shoot. How are you, anyway?"

I smiled back at her, but it was a strain. I wanted, as I often had for weeks, to simply let go and cry instead. Lynn was, after all, supposedly my best friend, if I could really consider any *girl* my best friend since Peter had come along.

"Fine," I lied, to break the tension. "How was *your* summer?"

"Oh, the usual. We were all at the cabin, driving each other crazy. My little sister has invented a bunch of new ways to torment me, and my mo——— uh, my parents just went off in the woods to commune with nature. You know, that bit."

"Why do you always go up there, if it's so miserable?" I started on my lock, but, as usual, I passed the second number twice and had to try again.

"What choice do I have? At least until I'm eighteen or whatever *they* think is a reasonable age to leave behind. I have to be kept away from the corrupting influences around here all summer, you know. Here — let me do that lock." She laughed quietly. "It's the one and only thing I ever seem to be able to do for *you*. Anyway, after a three-month dose of no dates, no television, no telephone, no nothing, I'll take corruption any day."

My locker opened. It seemed too empty, as it always did the first day, containing no hint of my two previous years of using it. Could have been anybody's, I thought.

"Peter bring you to school today?"

"Yes, he —"

"I met this dreamy guy this summer, but he told me I was too immature to take out. Big shot, huh? This school sure stinks, doesn't it? I hate being so close to the gym."

I did not try to answer or comment. When Lynn was nervous or excited, she often spoke this way, in Lynglish, as Mom used to call it. "She makes sense to herself, I suppose," Mom would say.

Lynn's face, after the long summer months, wasn't merely freckled — it was an explosion of pigment. And the flipped-up ends of her light brown hair looked brittle, tired of sun and water. My face, I knew, was paler than it had ever been at this time of year, and my hair drabber, no sunstreaks. The sun and I seemed to have been hiding from each other all summer.

Lynn was studying me, too, from head to toe. "Nice outfit."

"Thanks."

"It kinda surprises me, though. I guess I thought . . ."

"What? That I'd be wearing black or something?"

Lynn's eyes got all misty and sad-looking, but I had

22

seen her use this expression at times for effect. "Shoot, Mandy. I'm sorry. I'm — gosh, what can I say? I wish I knew the perfect thing to say. I really liked your — She was great." She looked close to real tears, and I felt guilty for having doubted her sincerity.

"That's okay, Lynn. I'm the one who should be apologizing. I'm sort of blaming everything on everybody today." My own tears pushed up, almost spilling. "I suppose everyone's going to look at me funny all day. To see what it's like to . . . you know."

Lynn shifted from one foot to another. Her purse strap looked worn to a string. "What . . . can I do, you know, to help?"

"Walk with me to band. Like always." I busied myself with my own purse, pretending to check for something before slamming shut my locker.

"You got it."

We headed for the opposite end of the school, where the band room was located; out of everyone's way, I had always thought.

"Say, Mandy," she said too loudly, too cheerfully, "did you hear about the new band teacher?"

"I heard Brunzar retired, that's all."

"Well . . ." Lynn rolled her eyes — completely clear and dry already — and wiggled her eyebrows meaningfully. Her recovery time was always about half anybody else's. "We've got this new young guy, Mr. Ekholt. They say he's a doll. Probably not much older than Peter, actually."

Hearing Peter's name made me flinch. Had I really

been that anxious to get rid of him only a few minutes earlier? I would call him after school. We could go out and, of course, end up parking somewhere. Thinking about the warmth of his arms made me wish I could call him immediately to apologize. But surely he must know what I'd been feeling.

The first day of school had always been a little tough for me. But nothing like this. I half expected an announcement over the loudspeaker: "Your attention, please. This is to remind you people to be especially kind to poor Mandy Smetana today. Give her your condolences and support. You can't miss her, she's the one with the long blue legs and the balloon arms." Suddenly I wanted to change clothes. What had made me buy this ridiculous outfit anyway? I longed for my comfy old corduroy jumper and knee socks.

Lynn was still chattering about the new band teacher. When we entered the dim instrument room that always smelled of spit, even after the summer, she shushed me unnecessarily and headed for the French horn shelf. I took my time putting my flute together, stopping to wrap my hands around the cold metal and breathing warmth into the mouthpiece. I had not practiced once all summer.

Lynn approached Mr. Ekholt immediately, amid the cacophony of instruments warming up, and used her French horn as an excuse — one of the valves was sticking. "Here, Mr. Ekholt," I could imagine her saying. "Please unstick me."

On her way past the flute section, up to her own, she

said, "He really does remind me of Peter. I'll bet he even plays the trumpet."

I could see why Lynn might think the new teacher was like Peter. The same dark hair and beard, the slender build. They both grinned a lot, too, and seemed to have nonstop music inside their heads and dancing hands. Mr. Ekholt looked around the room without meeting any of our eyes and tapped his baton lightly on his music stand. The room quieted enough for roll call and for a quick survey of the music arranged neatly in our folders. Mr. Ekholt leaned toward serious, classical music, I noticed with pleasure, but I could already hear the whining among others.

"Let's tune, please," he said, nodding to the eager, puckery-mouthed oboe player to whom we always had to tune our instruments. Tuning started with the one agreed-upon note but then degenerated into dissonant exploration. Mr. Ekholt tried to collect the scattering of notes into a C-major arpeggio but his face reflected the disbelief that fifty-some instruments could somehow find fifty-some different ways to play the same thing. My attempt was not any more on target than anyone else's.

Mr. Ekholt gave an embarrassed cough; he seemed to take it all too personally. For a moment he examined his wand as if it might be the culprit. Then he led us bravely into the first piece in our folders, and we followed.

That first rehearsal was such a disaster, it made me laugh afterward more than I had in months. An odd mixture of feeling good and awful sent tears rolling down my cheeks all the way to English, where I would part company with Lynn. She looked bewildered and worried about me.

"See you at lunch," I told her, and then hummed the last few raggedy notes of the Rimsky-Korsakov we had just butchered in band practice. She started to laugh too then, and we grabbed each other's arms for support. When the crowd of hurrying students had thinned out and we knew she would be late to her class, we didn't much care. We were still laughing and still crying, and I didn't want to go into my English class. I did not want to let go of her arm.

3 〜

I RECEIVED SO MANY compliments on my outfit all day, I couldn't decide if people felt sorry for me or if maybe I looked pretty good after all.

Tracy Anderson was in my math class, and she gave me a very friendly almost-hug. Tracy lived in an affluent part of town known as Oak Hills. She had invited me over to her house a few times, once with her best friend, Rachel. They had grown up together, and I remembered thinking how lucky they had been to have each other to play with every summer, while I had been working on our farm, for the most part alone. They both seemed to genuinely like me, but I didn't feel as if I fit in somehow.

"Mandy," Tracy said as we walked together from math to our last classes. "I'm sorry about your mother. I couldn't believe it when I heard. Are you okay?"

"I'm doing pretty well. Thanks."

"I never got a chance to meet your mom, you know. But I've heard she was something pretty special."

The familiar sting in my eyes returned full-force. "She was," I managed to say.

"I wish I'd met her. See you later." Tracy rushed ahead of me to her own class, her long pale ponytail swinging back and forth. Her walk was so sure of itself.

I was left with the sickening feeling that my not "fitting in" with Tracy and Rachel could have been more my fault than theirs. I had never even invited Tracy over, but from what she'd said about wishing she had met Mom, maybe she had been waiting for an invitation. After being in her impressive home, constructed of natural cedar and tucked into a great gathering of suburban oak trees, I just couldn't picture her in my house, an old farmhouse.

Maybe I was a snob in reverse. Something else to change this year? Invite friends over. New friends. Soon. Then they can finally meet . . . no. God, no. How come I keep forgetting about it, Mom?

Lynn was waiting at my locker after school. And so was Peter.

"Hi, Mandy," he said, his grin giving nothing away about the tension between us that morning.

Without really thinking about it, I greeted him by laying my cheek against his shoulder and waited for him to wrap his arms around me, books and all. He didn't let me down. "I'm sorry," I whispered.

Lynn hurried away with a quick "See ya." Once, she glanced over her shoulder at us.

"Rough day?" Peter said.

I reached over to open my locker, still leaning against him, but I kept missing that second number again.

"Here. Let me," he said. "21-3-7?"

"Right."

"What a memory, huh?"

I watched his steady hand turning the knob. He had thin, sinewy hands that sometimes, even after so much time together, could make me go all fluttery with a single touch.

"Thanks," I said when the lock clicked and he opened the door. Inside was a tall, thin purple box, waiting for me. Long-stemmed roses.

"I meant to get out of here before you got to your locker, to surprise you with these, but Lynn started talking and . . ."

I let go of the tears that had been threatening most of the day. They were different from those after band. Peter made them different, more of a release.

"And I'd say it's a darn good thing Lynn held me up. You'd never have gotten the stupid locker open." He gave me a tissue from his pocket. "The poor roses would have wilted to nothing in there before you ever saw them."

Time to laugh again. It felt so good.

"Mind if I take you home? You don't want to bring those home on the bus, do you?"

"No, I don't. Please, bring me home."

On the way to the parking lot, Peter started to put his arm around my waist and then changed his mind. "Hey, you want to drive today?" I realized how hard he was trying to do what I wanted, to be what I wanted him to be.

"Okay," I said. "I'll take us to Waldo's for a Coke. Maybe we can talk a little?" And park, I added to myself. There was something to be said for predictability.

*

While we were sitting, hunched over our Cokes, the words didn't come as easily as usual.

"Your dad seemed in pretty good spirits yesterday," Peter said at last. "That's . . . uh, that's why I asked him along, you know. People shouldn't be alone on holidays."

"I wasn't mad about that. I wanted him with us, at least for most of the day."

Peter nodded. "But it got to be too much. The two of us and you, huh?"

"Yes. Oh — you do understand, then. What a relief! In that movie, I thought —"

"Your dad understands too. We talked about it today. How you hate possessiveness."

"What? When?" The resentful, invaded feeling started to creep into me again. I hated it, but I couldn't seem to stop it lately. "You mean you came over while I was at school and discussed how to handle me?"

He gave me a weary look. "No, no, no. That's not what I meant. I was trying to help. Your dad's had a hard time, and he needs *both* of us."

"Meaning I'm not doing enough for him, right?"

"Meaning *nothing*, except what the hell's the matter with you lately?"

I finished my Coke, and we stared at each other for a while.

Nodding and lifting his palms into the air, Peter finally said, "Come on, then. I'll take you home. I can drop you off at the end of your driveway if you like."

Back in his car, which was filled with the scent of my

roses, I stopped his hand from turning the ignition. "Peter, I'm sorry. I want to talk about this. I really do. But I don't know how to explain to you why I get so angry at you for . . . for being here, I guess. I know that sounds crazy. Maybe I'm going crazy."

His fingers let go of the key and found my hand, which must have felt icy and stiff. "It may not make sense to me, but I do understand more than you think. I know you, craziness and all." His fingers let go of my hand and dropped gently onto my left thigh, which he began to stroke. "Did I tell you, by the way, how cute you look in that skirt?"

"Yes, in a way. But you also said you hated it."

"Oh, I hate it for other people to see. It's fun for *me* to look at, though." He smiled and turned my face toward his. We stayed that way for a long time, kissing, even though we were in a public parking lot and it wasn't dark yet.

It occurred to me that we were getting careless about this sort of thing. We had never even figured out what exactly we would do if, at the end of one of our dates, my dad stopped snoring suddenly and appeared in the living room, where we lay on the couch. We should run a drill sometime, I thought, timing ourselves, gathering together discarded clothing and runaway emotions, at least enough to pass Dad's unexpected scrutiny. I couldn't imagine how he might receive my nimble reassurance: but Dad, we *don't* go all the way. Maybe he wouldn't believe me.

It was starting to get darker now. The parking lot was

quiet, respectful. Peter unbuttoned my blouse and dipped his hand into the flimsy cup of my bra as swiftly and easily as if it belonged there.

Thoughts of my mom invaded suddenly, of her once-healthy, full breasts, how one and then the other had been removed and still the cancer had eaten away at her. I felt myself go limp in Peter's arms.

"What is it?" he mumbled into my neck.

"Nothing. Just hold me. Keep touching me there."

"Come on. What were you thinking about a few minutes ago? You were frightened of something."

"It was nothing. Just . . . nothing I want to talk about."

Peter pulled away from me slightly. "You used to tell me what was on your mind. Always."

"No, I didn't. How could I? How could anybody?"

His hands tensed on me, and I tried to reassure them with my own. His mouth covered mine again, and I didn't try to explain anything more. Lately, words seemed to get in the way.

*

It was nearly suppertime when I got home. I wondered, guiltily, what Dad and I would have to eat. Peter did not walk me to the door, even though I asked him to come in.

"Gotta go," he said. "I'll call you tomorrow night."

I hurriedly tried to figure out what I'd tell Dad about supper, how I might convince him that I'd had a plan in mind all along and that's why I'd known he wouldn't mind if I was late. An image of the chaotic kitchen, the way I had last seen it that morning, made me cringe.

I remembered opening the door in past years, home from school late, and being greeted by the most savory smells from our kitchen. Then I would hear my mom's tuneless humming with my dad's low voice underneath it and my brothers' erratic, sometimes bumptious voices in between as they related their triumphs or concerns to her. However, she had always seemed to be waiting especially for me, to hear mine as well.

The house was dim except for the kitchen. "Dad — sorry I'm late."

"Hello there," he said. "I've got to admit I was getting just a little worried about you. Well . . . not *worried*, exactly." He seemed flustered. "I trust you, and all that." Trying not to stare at my miniskirt, he added, "Dinner's nearly ready."

It seemed to me Peter had indeed been talking to him. "I was with Peter," I said.

"Oh, good. After last night and this morning, I wasn't sure if that was — I mean . . ." He could no longer stop himself from staring disapprovingly at my legs.

"Don't worry, Dad. I won't be wearing this again. It wasn't comfortable anyway."

"Oh? Good." He motioned for me to look around the kitchen. "What do you think?" Everything was reasonably clean, there was evidence of a few new groceries and something was simmering on the stove. He smiled at me.

"I think you've been very busy." I was careful not to act too surprised, but his efforts really were astonishing. He had not had such a good day since the week in August when my brothers had been with us and Sam's wife had announced she was having a baby at the end of winter. Dad had immediately thrown himself into a thorough housecleaning, almost as if the baby might arrive any day and criticize Grandpa's sloppiness.

This time I guessed I'd have to give Peter the credit for Dad's mood.

"Doesn't it smell good in here?" he asked.

"Yeah. What is it? Spaghetti sauce?"

"Well, it's from a jar, but it's supposed to taste like homemade. What pot do we use to boil the spaghetti? Do you know?"

Between the two of us, we managed to put together a pretty good supper, the best in weeks. While we ate, I told him about my new classes, leaving out anything that might spoil his cheerfulness, such as the fact that my new English teacher had given us the inevitable, dreaded assignment of writing about our summer vacations. "Last summer," I wanted to write, "my mother died. Fill in the rest for yourself."

"How's Lynn doing?" Dad asked.

"Oh, pretty well, I guess. I'm thinking about making some new friends this year, though. In addition to Lynn. I might be inviting some girls over soon. Maybe for overnight. Is that okay?"

He looked at me, alarmed. "Here?"

"Of course, here. Where else?"

Dad's eyes wandered around the kitchen. At last, he nodded.

"Thanks."

Dad left the table to get our dessert, and by then I had run out of things to say. He piled two bowls full of chocolate ice cream and then sat down to eat his as though fascinated by the way it melted on his tongue, slid down his throat. I did the same; there's nothing more quiet, I thought, than eating ice cream.

"Does this . . . this place bother you at all?" he asked finally, gazing around again.

"What? You mean this house?"

He gave me what appeared to be a nod.

"Well, not really. Why?"

He didn't answer.

"It's a nice house," I said. "Old, but nice."

"It's more than old," he said. "It was already old when I was born in it. I guess it's only natural for me to feel . . . an unusual attachment to it."

"Of course."

"And I . . . I guess, I wonder how you feel about it."

I couldn't quite figure out where this conversation was leading. Feeling like a confession might be in order, I said, "I used to be embarrassed by it, when I was a kid —"

"So many things have happened in this house."

"— but I've outgrown that now."

"Sometimes," he continued, "I hear things in these rooms. I hear the boys upstairs fighting over something, and I go up there and the room is empty."

I started clearing the table. Sam and Greg had not lived at home for years.

"And then I hear you in your room, singing your dolls to sleep. Singing yourself to sleep."

I flinched. "Dad —"

"But then I go in there and *your* room's empty too.

This room, this damn kitchen, is the worst. I hear her in here. She's as much a part of this room as that old stove over there."

"I know, Dad." I was pleased that our talk had turned to Mom. Now we're getting somewhere, I thought.

But he stared at me, his gaze the palest, coolest of blues, icy on my skin. "No, you don't."

I nodded vigorously. "Yes, I do. She's —"

"Don't you feel how empty these rooms are?"

"Dad, listen." I grabbed his arm. "I'm so glad you brought this up. Because I hear Mom all the time. We talk. She's —"

"I've heard you." His expression was stern, and I wasn't sure exactly why. Hadn't he just said he heard her too?

"She's everywhere," I continued. "Not just in this kitchen. Sometimes it's . . . it's like . . . almost like she never —"

"No." He withdrew from my grasp and lowered his eyes. "It's not like that at all." His thumbnail scraped at a callus on his forefinger; it was such a small movement and yet it seemed to me that it crowded everything else out, every other possible movement for either of us.

As we sat there, I realized that it wasn't the same for him after all. If he heard Mom, it was only echoes. That was fine for him, but it couldn't be for me.

My ice cream had melted into a smooth unappetizing mound. I swallowed several times to try to clear the way for it, but ended up taking it to the sink and rinsing it down the drain with hot water.

The silence was no longer tolerable. "Did I tell you,"

I asked loudly, whisking a few tears from my face with one hand, "that Peter brought me some roses today?" I rinsed and arranged our few dishes in the dishwasher and filled the saucepan to soak. "Here, I'll show you." I ran back to the dining-room table, the drop-off place, to get my flowers. "Pretty, huh?"

Dad looked at the roses and then quickly looked away again. He cleared his throat. "Your turn to do the dishes," he said and retreated into the living room to watch TV.

"I'm doing the . . . damn . . . dishes," I said to myself. Rinsing out a dishrag and squeezing it nearly dry, I poked it into random corners and rearranged objects on countertops.

I wished Dad and I could have gotten through the whole evening as well as it had started. Flowers. Why had I shown him the flowers? I should have known Dad would associate them with Mom. Not just from the funeral; in earlier, happier days, they had symbolized her recovery from surgery. She had gone a little nuts over flowers, actually. Planting dozens of them, bringing more into the house than it could gracefully display.

But the cancer had spread anyway. Breast surgery one summer, again the next, more panic, but no surgery the summer after that. Her death had seemed to be slow, and yet, looking back, I couldn't quite shake the sense of suddenness.

I could still feel the dull, unspecific pain I had felt in my own body whenever I had sat with Mom in the hospital. She always claimed that the drugs kept her comfortable enough, but Dad and I knew better. We could see her pain and feel part of it — no matter how small or useless — as our own.

We had talked only once about Mom's pain, Dad and I. It was about a week before she died, during one of our porch talks. Our glassed-in front porch was the kind of place that at dusk, with all the windows wide-open, allowed a slow, peaceful surrendering of the day. If Dad and I tended to exchange few words, hide our feelings from each other, that porch from dusk on into darkness offered an opportunity to make up for it.

In that one talk we discussed pain, all different kinds. And he told me how it had been when Mom had given birth to my brothers and me.

"They kept me away from her the whole time," he said, "as though she had some horrible, contagious disease. Or maybe they thought I did. Anyway, even halfway across the building from her, I felt her pains with her. My belly tightened and knotted up every few minutes, and then every few seconds, and sweat poured out of me. It was embarrassing. The nurses stared at me."

"Which of us was this?"

He thought for a moment. "Could've been any of you. Or maybe all three. I'm not too clear on that. But I do know that the pains finally stopped suddenly and, sure enough, it wasn't long before they came to tell me about our new baby."

"Dad," I said, "I think you're pulling my leg."

He shook his head and said, "Your mom said the same thing. She never did quite believe me, I don't think. But it didn't matter. I felt what I felt. It helped me get

38

through it. Gave me something . . . I don't know. Something to do."

He did not, that night or any other time, say the same thing was happening to him with Mom's cancer pain. But I think that's what he had meant to say. Mom's doctor told me to be careful what he ate because his blood pressure had shot up so alarmingly. "Pain does that," the doctor had said.

I tried to sort through my feelings about Dad while I cleaned the kitchen that autumn night. He had marched through the ceremonial parts of Mom's death with dignity and strength, inspiring me and my brothers to do the same, or try to. It was during those dreadful, tight-lipped and stiff-backed few days that I clung to *him*. I seemed to need the actual physical presence of his arms and shoulders within reach at all times. And when Dad wasn't able to comply, Peter did. I leaned shamelessly, cried until I thought my entire body would dry up into a husk and simply float away while nobody was looking.

Then two things happened simultaneously — Dad began to crumble and to take his turn at leaning, and I began to talk to Mom and replenish my strength through her. Peter helped Dad in the fields; I did all the housework, cooking, and the management tasks that Mom had always done. It didn't surprise anyone that it took three of us to do what the two of my parents alone had managed for thirty years. After all, Mom was no ordinary person.

I passed our porch on my way upstairs to do my homework, and I wished I could take Dad out there for one of our talks, like long ago. But that might have made him cling to me more. No, Peter had made some progress with him — Dad was trying hard to let go of me, and I would have to trust him to keep trying.

My part would simply be to act more independent and sure of myself, to take charge of *me*, even at the risk of losing Dad's approval now and then. I loved him so much, it might have been easier to give in and take care of him. But I knew that wouldn't be right for either of us.

"Good night, Dad," I said on my way upstairs. I held my roses in a vase behind my back, but he was already asleep in his easy chair. His mouth was open and his snores grew in volume to drown out the TV voices.

I didn't turn off the set because I knew the silence would only wake him up. It occurred to me that if he was bothered by empty rooms, then his bedroom was the last place he should be.

4 ⬿

AFTER THAT FIRST DAY I was back to my old clothes
even if not back to my "old self." I tossed the
miniskirt onto a shelf, saving it for Halloween; Lynn was
going to lend me a long black wig so I could be Cher,
and she would dress up as Sonny Bono.

"Hi, Babe," she said for the umpteenth time since
she'd come up with this brainstorm. It was Friday, and
we had met as usual at our lockers after school. "Gosh,
this is going to be great, isn't it? Sonny and Cher. Now
if we can just find the right party to go to. I've heard
Shelley Bingham gives the best ones. You know her,
don't you? The tall, gorgeous number who sat in back
of you last year in study hall? Neat girl, really. We might
go to modeling school together next year."

"Modeling school? Don't you have to be taller to —"

"Anyway, I'll finagle us into her party. Peter, too, of
course."

"He's not big on Halloween parties, you know. He —"

"I know. I know. It's kid stuff. I don't blame him.
You two will probably find some other, neater thing to
do."

41

"No, that's not what I —"

"Listen. I also heard Shelley's older brother's dreamy. Maybe I can get to know him then, huh?"

"I doubt you'll attract him dressed as Sonny Bono."

"Nonsense. He'll be fascinated. See you later." Lynn left me by my bus to start her walk home. "Bye, Babe." She broke into a slightly off-key rendition of "I Got You, Babe," which I knew would stick in my mind, uninvited.

As usual, Lynn left me a bit breathless, unable to complete my thoughts out loud. They would end up stunted or, worse, forgotten altogether. Dad had always liked Lynn. "Sweet girl," he'd say. "Bubbly." But Mom had been more perceptive. "She means well. She has a lot of love to give and a lot of joy. But she's not exactly a deep thinker, is she?"

Somehow, I had never cared about that before. I was enough of a "thinker" for both of us, and I liked that arrangement. Lynn had been comfortable in a way, demanding only what I could give naturally. But I could tell now that along with everything else, my friendship with Lynn was altering. Her needs seemed foreign to me all of a sudden; my own seemed stronger and more boisterous. I knew I might end up scaring her away.

Friendship had never come easily for me. I tended to rely on one relationship and let other people think what they wanted to about me. It was their problem if I seemed shy or stuck-up or dumb or self-satisfied or whatever, right? I had always watched Mom's way with people and admired it, but I knew it couldn't be mine. She was everybody's friend, it seemed. I was a friend to a particular few. When I started seeing so much of Peter, I felt my meager desire for girl friends dwindle even further. What more could I have needed?

The phone was ringing when I got in the house, sounding as though it had been ringing a long time, waiting for me.

"Hello?"

"Mandy? Thank goodness you're finally home." It was Lynn. Her voice was shaky. No more "Hi, babe."

"What's the matter?"

"Can you get away with the car?"

I checked the yard. "Well, it's here all right. I should ask Dad, though. When did you have in mind?"

"Right now. Couldn't you just leave him a note? Your dad always lets you take it as long as he's not using it. Please, it's important, or I wouldn't bother you."

"Where are you? What's happened?"

"You know that new steak place a couple miles north of town? On Highway 5?"

"What are you doing there? That's miles from your house."

"I know. That's why I need you." She hung up abruptly as I waited, stupidly, for further explanation.

As soon as I put down the phone, it rang again. "Lynn? What's going on? I'm —"

"Hi," Peter said. "How ya doing?"

"Fine, but . . ." A panicky feeling rose up from my stomach and settled just below my throat. I swallowed hard. What, I wondered, was Lynn up to? If she had just been stranded somehow, why would she have been in such a hurry?

"When should I pick you up tonight? Want to see a movie, or what?"

"I can't tonight, Peter. I have to go, uh — it's Lynn. She's in some kind of predicament again."

"Oh?" He paused a moment. "Well, I'll help."

"No. I mean, I don't *need help.*" I hadn't meant to shout, but I was getting more frightened for Lynn by the moment.

I heard Peter take a long drag on a cigarette and then exhale harshly. The sound gave away his impatience even if his words would not.

"Peter, the concert's tomorrow night, right? I'll see you then. Okay?"

"Sure. Seven o'clock."

"Bye, Peter."

He didn't answer and neither of us hung up.

"This is something I have to do," I said. "Alone."

"I understand." Another exhale, this one more even. "Bye, then."

"Bye." Still he didn't hang up.

I checked the kitchen clock and toyed with the idea of asking him over for later. Maybe 9:00. But no, I would see him the next night. That was settled. I hung up, left a quick note for Dad ("I'm going to Lynn's. Call me there if you need the car. Leftover chicken in fridge."), grabbed the car keys and ran outside.

*

Lynn was not in sight when I got to the steakhouse. My stomach churned and ominous words like *kidnapping*

44

flashed in my mind. But I found her in the ladies' room, looking about ten-years-old. "What on earth are you doing here?"

"Mandy, did you see a guy out there in a dark green army jacket, a tall blond guy?"

"I don't know. How could I —?"

"Go look, *please*. I'll explain on the way home. Just make sure he's gone first."

I checked out the nearly empty dining room and then returned with my report. "No one like that out there."

"Okay. Let's go."

"Lynn, this is ridiculous. Tell me what's —"

But she was already out the door, perhaps to escape the look I was giving her.

On the way to her house, she was quiet until she suddenly blurted it all out. "I know I shouldn't hitch-hike. I know that. But this guy stopped and he was so cute. He looked harmless. I got into his car right by the school, and we came here. He said he was hungry, hadn't eaten all day."

She scanned the road ahead and behind us, then settled back into the seat. "Well, he turned out to be a nut case. You should've heard the things he said to me when we got to that steakhouse. The most disgusting —"

"Lynn, if he'd intended to . . . intended something awful, why would he have taken you to such a public place?"

She gave me a stricken look, and I wondered why I was doubting that she had been in real danger. Would I have been more satisfied with her story if her clothes had been ripped, her skin bruised? "What I mean is," I said gently, "you were lucky he didn't drive you off to some secluded spot. Why a restaurant, do you suppose?"

"I told you — he was hungry. He probably didn't figure I'd hide in the bathroom all that time. I think he had me pegged for a real 'good time,' you know what I mean?" She shuddered. "I just wanted a ride, that's all. My legs were stiff from gym — all those calisthenics this week — and he was so cute. Shoot. Mandy, do I *look* like that kind of girl, the kind he thought I was?"

I examined her face, the freckles, the round eyes, the pouty mouth. Something about her tugged at me. For years I had wanted simply to take care of her. "You look . . . hungry," I answered at last.

She rolled her eyes. "Well, there. See? I was hungry, like he was. A cheeseburger sounded like just the thing."

I didn't bother to explain to her that I had meant a different kind of hunger. We had reached her house, and I kept the car running.

Looking down at her fidgety hands, Lynn mumbled, "Can you come in for a while? Are you busy?"

"No, I'm not busy." I felt strangely pleased, almost proud, to be able to say that. The evening was mine.

She looked at me, surprised. "Great. That's super." Grinning sheepishly, she added, "Sometimes I don't know what I'd do without you."

"Oh, I suspect you'd manage all right." I gave her an encouraging smile.

"Mandy, you're my best friend. Absolutely. I don't care what Shelley Bingham says about you. She's just

46

jealous. Hey, you want to stay for dinner? I don't know what Mom . . . I mean, what we're having."

"Lynn, you can say the word *mom* in front of me. Honest."

She blushed.

"I'd love to stay for dinner. Your mom's a great cook. I'll call Dad, but I'm sure he'll say it's okay." I had a nagging urge to ask what old Shelley What's-her-name had said, but I suppressed it. It didn't much matter.

We got out of the car and as she opened the front door, a blast of fragrant, oven-heated air hit us. "Bread," Lynn said, inhaling and grinning. "Mom's been having one of her bread days. Therapy, she calls it. Hey, you can try on that wig tonight. You want to help me put my Sonny costume together?"

"Honestly, Lynn. Halloween is weeks away."

"I know. But time flies. Don't you just love the smell of baked bread, though?"

I nodded contentedly as we closed the door and left the cold air behind it.

It wasn't until much later, after gorging on warm bread and then dinner, and then popcorn less than an hour after dinner, that it occurred to me that I *should* have been with Peter instead. But that feeling, that I should have, troubled me. I did miss him, it was true, but why that feeling of obligation, maybe even guilt, for having a good time without him?

I caught Lynn staring at me about this same time and, eerily, she said, "You miss him, don't you?"

"Lynn, what am I going to do?"

I was surprised and pleased when she needed no explanation about my question.

"Why, you'll marry him, of course."

A simple question, a simple answer.

5 ⟿

PETER PICKED ME UP for our date Saturday night in great spirits. The concert was the fourth in a series called Jazz at the Guthrie, all of which we had seen together. Tonight it would be Gerry Mulligan, one of Peter's favorites. We pulled out of my driveway and headed for the highway that would take us into Minneapolis.

"Mulligan's great," Peter said. "You'll really love him. He does some pretty superhuman things with that sax."

"With that what?" I giggled. All day I had been feeling rather giddy, out of control, but pleasantly so. The freedom I had felt the night before had ended up, unexpectedly, arousing me, and I was determined now to have fun.

"Sax," he answered. "What did you think I — Oh."

"Sorry. I didn't misunderstand on purpose."

"Yes, you did. I've always known the truth about you. You're a real *sax*-fiend."

"I don't know what you mean." I slipped my right hand inside his suit jacket and rubbed him along his side.

He squirmed. "Cut it out. I know you're not crazy about jazz, but I had no idea you'd resort to this to keep us from getting there."

"Resort to what?" I started unbuttoning his shirt, slowly. It was starched down the front, making it easier to slip the buttons out one-handed.

"Okay, kid, you asked for it." He swerved suddenly off the road, stopped the car and started tugging at my clothes, making beast noises. His beard on my skin raised goose bumps.

I shrieked and tickled him back. It was an old and wonderful game. But at some point he started getting serious. "Wait, Peter." I realized I'd been teasing him in a way I hadn't meant to, not exactly.

His movements had slowed, and he was silent. His hands and mouth were searching, alert.

"Peter, stop kidding around. Really, we'll be late."

He pulled away, buttoned his shirt and straightened his tie, all without looking at me. "Okay. Let's go. You're right. Sorry." He started up the car again.

Several minutes passed. Something about his face, his expression as he drove distractedly, prompted me to blurt out a question I had wanted to ask for months. "Peter? Have you ever . . . uh, you know, actually done it, with a girl?"

"What? God, you are in a strange mood tonight. What did you have for supper, an aphrodisiac?" He turned on the radio and started drumming on the steering wheel with his fingertips.

I switched off the radio. "Aren't you going to answer me?"

He sighed. "What was the question again?"

"You know very well what I asked. I think I have a right to know. After all, we're practically . . . I mean, we've come pretty close a few times."

"Mandy, come on. What's it to you what I've done, what I did before I met you, which was nothing anyway?"

"What about last year? In New York. You were at Juilliard a whole term — plenty of time to go out with someone."

"Well, you had plenty of time too."

"Stop changing the subject. Answer my question."

"Yes. Okay, yes. Once. Satisfied?"

"With who?"

"What difference does it make, with who? Nobody you know. Nobody I care about."

"You made love to her and you didn't care about her?" I was strangely fascinated by all this. It occurred to me that I should be jealous. "You don't have to lie to me. You must have cared."

"Yes. No. I mean, I thought I cared before, but then, as it turned out, I didn't. Don't."

"You're talking funny, you know that?" I said. "Why does this make you so nervous?"

"Wouldn't it make you nervous?"

"I don't know," I said. "I've never done it. I think it's pretty gross, though, if you didn't care about her. What was she, some sort of tramp?"

"No, of course not. She was a violinist."

"A violinist? At Juilliard?"

"No, a violinist at Yankee Stadium. Of course, I met

her at Juilliard. She was good too." He added quickly, "A good violinist. She'll be a concert soloist before long."

"Gee, maybe we can go see her someday. Wouldn't that be fun?"

"Now you're getting that snotty tone of yours," Peter said. "You started this whole conversation, not me. If you don't want to know something, don't ask. Let's drop it. We're here."

I admired the Guthrie as we approached it from the parking lot. The building, at night, always made me think of a large, rectangular glass box, lit up from the inside by some magical source. Maybe churned out by all the people on its many different levels. I checked how I looked in a window before we entered, wondering if I would ever feel I belonged in this wonderful place. After several plays and concerts, I still felt like a kid on a field trip, with my name and school name pinned to my coat.

The concert was exactly as I had expected. I had trouble with jazz, unlike most other kinds of music. The rather helter-skelter nature of it made me restless. The musicians would start with a tune or musical idea, often a familiar one. Then each one in turn would go off on his own individual trip with that same musical idea. I couldn't seem to follow their itineraries, and although I could appreciate their skill and applaud along with everyone else when each musician phased out in favor of the next one, I was always relieved when they returned "home" as a group.

Peter, of course, was enthralled. He grabbed my hand

at one point and squeezed it so hard he hurt me. I longed to share his enthusiasm. Possibly that violinist had.

We went to our favorite deli afterward. He could tell I hadn't exactly loved the concert, so he refrained from talking about it more than absolutely necessary. Over our corned beef on pumpernickel, we talked about school.

"How's that new guy, Ekholt, is it? How's he doing?" Peter munched on his sandwich.

"He's pretty good. You'd like his style. But he's so different from Brunzar that the band still seems to be in a state of shock."

Peter nodded. "I liked Brunzar. Always did."

"Well, of course, you did. You were his pet: 'Peter, my boy. Take over the dance band tonight for me, will you? Oh, and here's a half-dozen students for you.' "

Peter snorted and shook his head.

" 'And, Peter — go audition here next week, and there the week after. Here're your scholarship applications. I lined them all up for you.' He loved you, Peter, and your talent."

"What did *he* know?"

"You weren't exactly treated like that at Juilliard, huh?"

I watched him gaze around the room as if in search of distractions. "Let's not talk about this," he said.

"Peter, please. Why not? Why won't you ever talk about it?"

He filled his mouth with sandwich, but I took his plate away and waited patiently until he had finished chewing. "Say," he said after swallowing, "you never told me what lunacy Lynn was up to last night."

53

"Peter. Tell me about Juilliard now. All you did when you got home last Christmas was say you missed me and act like everybody should be thrilled that you weren't going back to New York."

"Well, that's true, Mandy." He placed his hand melodramatically over his heart. "I couldn't live without you."

I shoved his plate back to him. "Sure, sure. You were so lovesick you went to bed with the first girl you met out there."

His eyes grew serious. "It wasn't like that. Not at all. I did miss you. God, it was awful. But that was only part of it. I just didn't have the talent, okay? Is that what you want to hear? I washed out in one lousy term. Can you love a washout? I'll probably be another Brunzar or Ekholt now. Big deal, huh? Big talent."

"But you shouldn't feel ashamed. Most people don't get to go to Juilliard at all."

"I wanted it so bad, but I never should have gone." He seemed to have ignored my remark. "Here I've always felt on top of things, sort of looked up to. *There* I was the bottom of the heap. And I hated that feeling. Hated it." Peter pushed aside his half-eaten sandwich, stared at it, then at me. "I wanted to come back to you, but not like that."

The way he was looking at me made me uneasy. Perhaps he needed my reassurance that he was not a washout, that he was worthy of me and of others. I knew I didn't consider him a failure, but there had been plenty of times he had disappointed me. What about all those times I had disappointed him? How could he still love me so much? Was my tolerance so much lower, my capacity for love deficient?

"Peter," I blurted out, "I love you. I don't care what you've done or not done, or will do, with your life. I really do love you." Hearing those words in my own steady voice was as soothing to me as it must have been to him.

He surprised me by blushing slightly, then touched my hand. His face looked different to me, but I couldn't figure out why.

"Ready to go?" Peter's eyes made my stomach clench and then ease the way his embrace often did. I recognized the look on his face now: it was one of a starving man at a feast.

I found it surprisingly easy to return the look. And why not? I was starving, too, in much the same way.

"I sure wish I had that apartment now, don't you?" He stood behind my chair and placed his hand at the small of my back when I joined him. My breathing grew more rapid, and I knew my face must be flushed. It was a relief to enter the cool darkness outside.

The breeze, carrying its messages of chimney smoke and winter-ready trees gave us a welcome pause, a moment to collect our thoughts and regain control.

On the drive home, the songs on the radio provided a focus. When a Dylan tune began, Peter cupped an invisible harmonica to his mouth and then grimaced in comical agony as he sang along in a Dylanish whine.

When he broke off suddenly, I understood why; it was the words: "I want you . . . so-o-o bad."

"Peter," I said when he had stopped in our yard. "Can I ask you something?"

He put his arm around me. "Sure thing. Shoot."

"What was it like?"

"What?"

"With that violinist. What was it like?"

He pulled his arm away, buried his face in his hands and groaned. "You've gotta be kidding."

"I'm serious. I want to know."

He looked at me for a moment. "It was . . . not great."

"What do you mean?"

"Well, for one thing . . ." He grabbed the steering wheel as if for support and averted his eyes. "I was drunk at the time."

"You were?"

"We'd been at this party. And I took her home and well, all of a sudden, there we were — in her bed."

I waited for him to continue.

"Mandy, I honest-to-God don't remember much about it. I wasn't myself. I was so lonely. I think I pretended she was you. Until . . ." He laughed. "She started to hum."

"Hum? While you were making love?"

"Not just a little hum, a really forceful, musical kind of hum. Beethoven's Violin Concerto, I think it was. Yes, that much I remember. She'd been rehearsing it all day."

"That's kind of weird, isn't it?"

He shook his head slowly. "No more weird than my pretending she was you. It was all a mistake."

I nodded.

"Satisfied now? Say, listen, I've got an idea." He got out of the car and walked me to the front door of my house. "First, see if he's snoring all right."

I stuck my head in the door. "Yeah, he's in great form tonight," I whispered and closed the door again.

"Good. Now go in and wait for me. I'm going to park the car down below the hill and then, if he gets up for something, he'll think I've gone home."

"And where will you be?"

He kissed me gently on my lips, then my neck. "In your bed, with you, of course."

"Peter, come on. We can't do that."

"And why not?" He was still kissing me, and his hands were inching my skirt up toward my hips.

"Stop it," I said without conviction, but a panicky feeling expanded in my chest.

When he left me abruptly to go hide his car, my heart was pounding. It will work, I thought. Dad will never know. He never checks on me once I've gone to bed.

Peter's car was now out of sight and quiet. I heard his footsteps climbing the hill. He was walking very fast. Our yard-light lit his way once he reached the top of the hill. He was smiling, but his walk had a jitteriness about it.

Then he was surrounding me and blocking the light. Each spot that his hands touched came more alive than the rest of me, and I longed to have that aliveness fill me from the inside and spread to every inch of my body. I heard a small groan while we were kissing and I wondered which one of us was producing it, but it didn't really matter.

Air. I needed air so badly. "Peter," I managed to say. "I . . . can't . . . breathe."

He opened the door behind me and started gently but steadily pushing me through. My body resisted, feeling somehow leaden and yet light as air at the same time. His hands released the door for a moment to hold me tighter. "Please," he whispered directly into my ear.

The door shut with a muted sound that to my ears seemed to whisper back "No." I pulled suddenly away from him and sat down on the front steps, my arms wrapped tightly around my knees, and said, "No, Peter. I can't." The nerve endings of my skin quivered crazily. "I mean it. No."

He stepped a couple of feet away from me. I couldn't see his eyes because the light was glaring on the top of his head. "I love you, Mandy," he said quietly. "It's all right because I love you. I want to show you how much."

"It's not all right, because . . ."

"If you're worried about getting pregnant, I'll take care of that. That's for me to keep from happening."

His being "prepared" reassured and infuriated me at the same time. I shook my head vigorously.

"Why not? Tell me."

"Because, I'm not sure how I feel about you. I —

Sometimes I'm afraid I'm mixing up how you make my body feel with how I really feel, inside."

"What are you saying? You don't love me?"

"It's easy to love you, Peter. You're so . . . so comfortable to be with. I can be myself with you, talk to you."

"Comfortable, huh? All that talk tonight, about sex. What was all that about, if you didn't want —?"

"I was curious."

"Curious?" He started to pace, still a few feet away.

"Peter, I met you when I was just starting to understand . . . things, about my body. About love, too, of course. I do love you. You've been my best friend for —"

"Best friend? That's great." His pace was quickening. His hands were clenching and unclenching at his sides.

"Everything I've learned about how to feel, about responding and touching and . . . well, you know, I've learned from you. You've taught me so —"

"Taught! So now I'm your teacher *and* your best friend. Oh, and let's not forget 'comfortable.' Somehow, I thought I was more than that. Isn't that a laugh?"

"You are more than that. You're twisting my words —"

"And all those questions tonight. You weren't leading up to anything. You weren't even jealous. That was more teaching, wasn't it? Well, you'd better find yourself a better expert than I am."

For a moment I listened to him carefully, not trying to argue, just listening to his assessment of me and of our relationship. I almost nodded.

He was still pacing and still muttering. I strained to hear what he was saying. "Not only do I get to teach music instead of enjoying it, now I get to teach sex too. Wow! I'm really something, aren't I? Really something."

"I don't want it to be a mistake, that's all," I said as much to myself as to him. "Like it was with that violinist. It has to be the right time, with the right . . . with . . ."

"Go ahead, finish. With the right person. That's what you were going to say. So, what I've been is a friend, a buddy, to teach you so you can be ready when the *right person* comes along."

"No, that's not what I —"

"God, Mandy." He stopped in front of me. "I knew it could hurt. I knew you could . . . you could make me feel like a — But God." Then he crouched down near me so that his face was level with mine. "You know," he said, his voice a low monotone. "You've changed in the last few months. Really changed. I've tried to help. Maybe I tried too hard, I don't know. But . . . oh, never mind." He stood up and backed away.

I watched him get smaller and dimmer.

He paused and turned around. "No, I think I'll go right ahead and say it. Why not? It seems to me that if there was ever any part of you that was like your mother . . . well, it seems like it died along with her."

I closed my eyes and listened to his retreating footsteps. In a minute I heard his car start again. His headlights flooded the night briefly, and then he was gone.

I sat, numb, on the step. After a few minutes I started to shiver. But for once the tears wouldn't come. Not even one.

6 ~

THE NEXT MORNING I woke up with an aching sense of loss that, at first, I tucked away as having to do with Mom. Closing my eyes, I allowed myself to think about her and the scurrying she would be doing, since it was Sunday. She had been our church organist for years and loved it. But getting us all ready to go as early as she had to be there was an exhausting task. After facing the family's sleepy, hungry, and just plain ornery bickering, actually sitting down to work must have seemed a rest.

It wasn't until I started to get dressed for church that I remembered what had happened the night before. Sinking back into my bed half-dressed, I wondered if I wasn't mistaken. Had I actually done it — broken up with Peter? Was he gone?

If I could just call him to make sure, or maybe he'd be calling me later today. I struggled to remember what each of us had said and why. Then, from underneath the weight of fears and regrets, I discovered a tiny particle of reason: I had freed myself of a relationship that was no longer good for me. I had done the right thing, painful though it might be at the moment.

I stayed in bed, pretending to sleep in, so Dad would go to church without me. When I heard his car pull away from our driveway, I slipped into the quiet kitchen, hungry for a solitary breakfast. One shelf in the pantry contained cereals. Neither Dad nor I were cereal eaters, so the lineup of boxes was the same as it had been for my mother.

Pulling out a box, I couldn't help but smile at its appearance. We had an old family joke about Mom's strange but consistent inability to open packages properly. Cereal box tops were opened anywhere but along the designated lines, their inner bags savagely ripped open. Kleenex boxes appeared nibbled on by sharks. And she had been strictly forbidden to touch M&M bags, because the widely scattered results would end up underfoot for weeks.

Methodically, I tossed out each box of stale cereal and then checked the rest of the kitchen shelves, uplifted by such simple housecleaning. As each hopelessly violated package disappeared from sight into a large black bag, I felt better.

In one crumb-filled corner I discovered a bag of coconut that my mom had tried to repair with masking tape. I examined it for a moment, remembering the coconut topping on my last birthday cake. But the flakes felt hard as metal scrapings between my fingers, and it joined the others in the bag.

Throughout the house, I found more such packages. Reminders, certainly, nearly as much as the clothes and other personal belongings we had boxed up weeks earlier. But more than reminders, these packages containing Mom's unmistakable imprint represented a kind of loose end, the last straightening up that needed to be done.

When Dad returned from church, I was shocked to find that familiar imprint again — it was in his face, in the way he walked, the way he slipped off his suit coat. Dad was like one of Mom's exuberantly opened packages, and he appeared unable to repair the damage.

"Good morning," I said.

He looked around the kitchen, searching for something, and I realized I should have been cooking dinner. Even with her job at church, Mom had managed to prepare a large Sunday dinner. Usually it cooked while we were gone, to greet us when we returned. We all took it for granted — Mom worked magic. She could be in several places at once, and each place would seem exclusively her domain.

"Uh, I guess you're hungry, aren't you?" I was still holding the bulging garbage bag, which Dad now stared at. "This is just stale food and stuff. Let's see . . . there must be something around here I could make."

I found a couple of steaks in the freezer and scratched in vain at the frost with my fingernails. How long, I wondered, do these take to thaw?

We ended up eating pancakes and bacon. Dad seemed disappointed in me since I had thought ahead on other Sunday mornings during the summer and presented him with dinner. I wanted to explain about Peter, but I was sure he'd take Peter's side (unless I mentioned the sexual matter, which I never could, not with Dad). He had certainly defended Peter often enough before.

After dinner, Dad made motions to help with the dishes but ended up wandering off to read the paper. I knew I was not behaving as he needed me to behave that day. Peter's advice to him about not depending on me so much had apparently begun to fade.

The rest of the day, Dad and I avoided each other. He hid because I wasn't Mom, and I hid because he wasn't Mom either; never had that fact been so obvious to me as it was that Sunday after I broke up with Peter.

"Mom," I would have been able to say, "I know I've handled some things badly. I know I've been taking, taking, taking, from Peter and not giving enough. Do you think I love him at all?"

"Of course you do. As much as you can right now."

"Maybe I should have gone ahead and had sex with him." I knew what she would have said about that, but I couldn't resist testing her, seeing if, for once, she might overreact.

"Sex is an even more grown-up thing than love." Yes, she had told me that many times. "Peter should be able to understand your reservations as well as your needs, and *his* needs. He loves you," she would remind me. "Even if you're not quite grown-up yet, he loves you in a grown-up way."

Who am I trying to kid? I wondered. If Mom really were here to talk to me, maybe she would be furious at me for the way I'd treated Peter. She would agree that I was not ready for sex, but she could point out gentler ways of dealing with the issue than I had found.

My fantasy conversation could go nowhere; I needed Mom in person. So I imagined her gathering me up exactly as she had when I was littler and easier to gather, holding me against her chest and breathing deeply with me, maybe even matching her heartbeat to mine.

Just before going upstairs to bed that night, I was cornered by Dad. "What have you been moping about all day?" he asked. "Another fight with Peter?"

"I haven't been moping. Just thinking. I have lots on my mind right now. I have to decide —"

"You're going to lose him," Dad interrupted. "Then you'll be sorry."

"What do you know about it? What do you know about me?" A flood of tears burst through and I could barely see Dad sitting there, glum and accusing. I ran up the stairs, but he didn't follow, of course. Mom would have followed. Even if it was just to make me return to apologize.

I did return, to the halfway point of the staircase. But no apology emerged. "You don't care about me and what's good for me," I said. "You have to let go of me, but you can't."

I couldn't see Dad at all anymore but I sensed his rising to come after me. I sensed his anger and his hurt, and I ran upstairs, slammed my bedroom door, and waited. The silence in the house was unnatural. It was as if neither one of us existed anymore. But my mom's face was at hand, and it was moving. She was shaking her head, sadly. "No, no. . . ."

7 ～

MONDAY MORNING, at school, Lynn was flushed and in one of her extremely chattery moods that required very little response from me. For that, I was grateful.

"Guess who I ran into yesterday, at our church, of all places. We were putting on *The Music Man*. Well, not *we* exactly. I wasn't in it, but my little sister, the creep, got to be one of the kids in River City. If I hear that silly song about the Wells Fargo Wagon once more, I swear I'll rip her vocal cords out. . . . Anyway, guess who."

"I don't know."

"Charlie Linderman."

"Who?"

"Charlie. You remember. That guy Peter lined me up with, two summers ago, so we could double. Remember? When we . . ." She laughed and then covered her mouth to quiet herself. "We went to that hotel."

I sighed. Hotel? Charlie who? "Lynn, I'm sorry. I'm not following you."

She grabbed my arm and guided me toward the band room. "Yes, you do. It was just before school started, and it was so hot and I called you up and pleaded with you to do something with me so I could get away from my bitchy family because we were still unpacking. So you and Peter lined me up with Charlie. Peter knew him from somewhere or other. We went to dinner at that big, classy hotel downtown. And then we went swimming, right in the hotel pool. The 'Guests Only' pool. Remember?"

"Oh, yeah. *That* hotel. I thought you meant something — Well, anyway, now I remember Charlie." I smiled as I remembered sneaking in and jumping into that pool as if we owned the place; the cool slickness of Peter's body against mine, his grip on my ankle and then hand over hand up my leg. "That was fun."

"Fun? It was fantastic. The looks on those people's faces when we took off our clothes —"

"Come on, now. We had swimsuits on underneath."

"I know. But we sure weren't supposed to be there. And then, after we swam, we just bundled up our clothes and walked right through that cushy, carpeted lobby in our dripping swimsuits and out the door. Cool as can be. I thought I'd die laughing."

"Yes, but you didn't care much for Charlie, remember?"

"Didn't I? Well, he doesn't seem so bad now. Not yesterday he didn't. Gosh, Peter sure can think up some great things to do, though, can't he? You guys must have —"

"Wait a second," I said as we got to the band room. "That wasn't Peter's idea, going swimming after dinner in that place."

"Yes, it was."

"No, it was *our* idea — yours and mine. We called the guys up and told them to wear swimsuits under their clothes like we'd decided to do. Just in case."

Lynn scowled and shook her head. "Well, it doesn't matter. It was Peter who made it fun." She went off to her section of the instrument room and I leaned against my shelf, my stomach tight. Peter, Peter, Peter. I wondered if that was all anyone could think about around me. Peter and Mandy. A couple. A "thing." Two parts of a whole. Except I kept feeling my part getting smaller and smaller. And everyone else thinking that was great. If we eloped tomorrow, had ten kids in ten years, everyone would cheer. "Isn't that Peter something? Having all those kids. Wow!"

"Coming?" Lynn asked me, nudging me with the bell of her French horn.

"Sure." I put my flute together and followed her inside. Dozens of instruments were tuning up and going over tricky passages, clashing with others. It sounded like a madhouse supplied with horns and drums.

"Boy, are you in a mood today," Lynn said. She waited by my music stand, staring at me.

I forced my forehead to unpucker and my mouth to turn up, surprised at the effort it took. "Yeah, well." I shrugged. Be nonchalant, I told myself. "That's what happens when you break up with someone, I guess."

"What? You and Peter?" Lynn nearly dropped her horn.

Mr. Ekholt tapped his stand with his baton. "Quiet, everyone. To your seats."

Lynn backed away from me, the look on her face so comical, I smiled for real this time.

After practice, I skipped cleaning my flute so I could get away quickly and on to my next class alone. Lunchtime would be time enough to answer Lynn's questions. More self-defense, I thought. I could tell her most anything except the actual facts. The details. Those were nobody's business but Peter's and mine.

*

"Tracy," I asked on our way out of math. "Want to do something with me this weekend? Come over to my house maybe, on Friday?" We had been walking together from math regularly by that time. She was easy to talk to, especially about things political. I noticed that on the cover of her math notebook was sprawled the word *peace* in several different scripts.

Tracy hesitated a moment. "Friday? Well, I'm sorta free, but I'm surprised you are."

"Oh, Peter and I broke up." I shrugged again, getting better at it as the day progressed.

"No kidding? Hey, that's too bad. Join the ranks."

"Friday night, then?"

"Well, I'm usually with Rachel on Fridays, but . . ."

"Maybe she'd like to come too. And I'll talk to Lynn — you know her, don't you? We'll make it a party."

Tracy brightened. "That sounds good."

And, surprisingly, it did.

An hour later, after school, Lynn was still pumping me about Peter and I was feeling too good to bother with all that. I didn't remember until after I had left her and settled into my bus that I had intended to invite Lynn over on Friday too. Oh, well, I thought. I can call her as soon as I get home.

Dad was working out in the cauliflower patch when I got off the bus. I could see the small blue-shirted speck amidst the orderly rows of green. When I tried to phone Lynn, her mother said she was at her piano lesson but that she would be sure to have her call me when she got home.

Hearing a car approach the house, I checked automatically for the baby blue Chevy and then I remembered that Peter would not be around anymore. Hadn't I begun to feel okay about that earlier in the day?

Dad's truck lurched to a stop by the shed where we stored our produce until it was sold. He emerged from the cab, lifted his hat and wiped away sweat from his forehead with one sleeve. I was struck by how young he looked out there, lugging heavy baskets, moving in long, determined strides. His bare forearms were deeply tanned and muscular. His blue work shirt still hung a little too loosely from the weight he had lost, though, and he had to keep hitching up his pants.

I changed my clothes and went outside. When Dad saw me, he paused, then started unloading the truck again.

"Dad."

He straightened up and looked at me. His face wore a staring-into-the-sun grimace.

"I'm really sorry about last night. I . . . we . . . Peter and I broke up, you see. For good, I'm pretty sure of it. I was really a mess yesterday, but I didn't mean to take it out on you."

Dad nodded and stroked both of his cheeks with one hand, back and forth, then rubbed his chin. He clearly couldn't think of the right thing to say, afraid to say the wrong words, such as "You'll make up with him right now if you know what's good for you."

I decided to help him unload. Many times in recent summers we had shared an unspoken respect and affection for this kind of work, ever since the time I was fourteen and had helped him pick the melons. His back had gone out on him, Mom was in the hospital and a severe hailstorm was hurrying our way. We had saved those beautiful, perfect cantaloupes together and talked about them, and about other things, well into the night.

I knew that something as simple as working together would not fix our relationship, but then I didn't want the broken pieces replaced the way they had been, anyway. Some restructuring and rearranging needed to be done, and unloading the truck side by side seemed a healthy start.

We decided on a supper of BLTs, fresh but overgrown beans and potato chips. Silence hovered over the table as we ate, but it was not a hostile silence, more a restful one. By the time Dad headed for the television and I prepared to do my homework, I think we were both breathing easier.

Lynn did not call me back that evening. Maybe she had somehow heard about my inviting other girls over to my house and thought she would not be included. That was just the kind of snub she might never forgive me for; I had not had *her* over in ages.

What, I wondered, was happening between Lynn and me? I struggled to remember the fun we'd had together over the years and it did seem that we had laughed a lot and talked plenty, but I wasn't sure how much we had actually shared. I had no idea what she wanted to do after graduating — except for her recent remark about going to modeling school with Shelley — and I was sure she didn't have the slightest idea what I wanted from life either. Except, of course, for marriage. We had discussed getting married and having kids for hours on end since we had been in elementary school.

With Lynn, I had tried to straighten out some of my confusion about sex. Between the two of us, pooling the considerable information we had received from our mothers (mostly mine), we figured we had come to a reasonably good understanding of what it was all about.

"Mandy," Lynn had said once years ago, "now you pretend you're a boy and I'll be me."

"Which boy?"

"Any boy."

"Okay," I said with a giggle, "how about Frankie Landers?"

"Ugh! Don't be gross, Mandy. Please, this is serious."

"Okay, I'm Paul Newman."

"No, that'll make me too nervous. Just be a boy, any nice boy. My very first real boyfriend."

I nodded and we sat close together on the window seat in her bedroom, giggling. "This is a car," she said, trying so hard to be serious. Since I was usually the one to initiate games, she was using a more assertive voice, trying on something new to her character. "We are parked in a car after a date."

"Okay." I was enjoying following her lead for a change. We sat.

"So, do something already!" she shrieked at me.

"Okay," I said again. I put my arm awkwardly around her shoulders. "Oh, wait now. Was I supposed to hold your hand first?"

"Probably, but never mind. And you don't have to really kiss me, either. It's the words that are important. Just pretend you're incredibly turned on by me."

Tightening my grasp, I started pushing her down. "Kiss me. Kiss me. I love you. I want you."

Lynn struggled meekly against me, pretending to push back at me, and then swooned. "Oh-h-h. Take me. I'm yours."

I sat up. "What? Why'd you say that?"

She bent her legs and curled up in a ball. "Why not?

"Well . . . because . . ." I searched for the answer. "Because we're not married, are we?"

"If we were married, smarty, what would we be doing parked in a car?"

"This is like a first date, isn't it? He's testing you, to see how far you'll go."

"Gosh, Mandy. What was I supposed to do? Girls

73

only slap boys' faces in the movies. Get with it — haven't you heard about frigidity?"

"Lynn, you don't have to give in to a boy if you don't love him. Sex is very special, and it should be saved."

"Mandy, you're hopeless. You'd better grow up before we get to high school."

I smiled now, thinking back to those two scrawny, flat-chested kids sitting together on a window seat. We had grown a lot since then, each in our own stubborn direction, listening to each other less and less, especially about boys. At the moment, I wondered which of us had grown up more.

8 ⚘

C OME ON, LYNN," I said Friday, after school. "How many times do I have to ask you? Please come to my house tonight. I meant to ask you right away and you know it. Stop being so pigheaded."

I wanted to add, and mean it, "I need you there," but if Lynn was going to be so touchy just because I had been a little late in inviting her (and Tracy had mentioned my invitation to her right after school that day), then I could live without her at my house. Hadn't the whole idea been to start *new* friendships anyway?

Lynn gave me her patented I'm-hurt-but-don't-care look as she opened her locker. "I told you, Mandy. I've made other plans for tonight. Honest. Shelley and I are going to see *Butch Cassidy and the Sundance Kid.* I've heard it's about the greatest movie ever."

"It's good. But you can see it anytime."

"You've seen it already?"

"Well, yes."

"Oh, shoot. Just once I'd like to see a movie before you do."

"You saw *Funny Girl* before I did last year."

"Big deal. I saw it with my parents. I had to — it was my birthday, and they thought they were doing something neat for me."

"So what?"

"So, I missed most of the movie because I kept watching out for people I knew and hiding from them. Who wants to be caught at a movie with your parents? Four rows behind us Ben and Judy were making out like crazy. I could *hear* them, for crying out loud. It was horrible. I kept waiting for Dad to turn around and start lecturing them about teenage morality."

Abruptly she changed the subject. "Have you heard from Peter lately?" she asked.

"No." I looked at Lynn and something in her eager freckled face reminded me that we were friends and that I should act like one. "Actually, Lynn, I have to admit, I halfway hope it's him every time the phone rings, and I still watch for his car. I guess I've got to be about the most mixed-up — "

"You're an idiot, if you ask me."

"Lynn! Thanks a lot."

"I mean, letting a guy like that slip through your fingers. And why? Because you're a prude. That's why."

"How do you know anything about what happened. I never said it had anything to do with sex."

"It's obvious. At least to me. I know you, Mandy, and the way I figure it, you started letting all those useless guilt feelings get in the way of your having a good time and you started telling Peter you didn't want to do it anymore. Naturally, he split."

76

I glared at her, but resisted the urge to straighten her out on what happened. If that's what she wanted to think, who cared?

I tried my lock for the fifth time — it always fought me when I was upset.

Lynn started to reach over to help me, but I glared at her and she left me to do it for myself. "Have fun tonight," she called over her shoulder, "with your Oak Hills buddies."

Tracy and Rachel had planned to meet at my locker so we could catch my bus together. I started to panic, because even after all the time I had wasted at my locker, they weren't in sight yet. If we missed my bus, I'd have to call Dad to come get us.

Finally I saw a commotion at the other end of the hall. They were running awkwardly with overnight suitcases and sleeping bags banging into the other students they passed. There was something odd about the way they glanced at each other and avoided touching as though they had been arguing too.

"Hey, Mandy. Are we late?" Tracy called out, forcing a smile. She was by far the taller of the two, her long legs flashing under a faded denim skirt, and her straight ponytail swinging over one shoulder.

"I was beginning to wonder if you were going to make it, that's for sure," I said.

"We wouldn't have missed it for anything," Rachel said, pushing in front of Tracy. Her round face transformed itself into one of the comical expressions for which she was famous schoolwide. This one was a leer. "I hear you got something special cooked up for tonight. Men, maybe? In leather jackets?"

I laughed. "No, I'm afraid about all we'll be cooking up is pizza and popcorn."

Tracy was glaring at her friend. "Men in leather jackets? My gosh, where's your mind lately?"

"I don't have one, remember? Not up to your standards, at least."

"We have to hurry." I grabbed a sleeping bag, and we ran. The bus was beginning to make its move out of the line when we reached it, all of us panting now. The kids on my bus stared at us as we pushed our bulky way through the doors and dropped, exhausted, into seats.

Almost a third of the bus was emptied at the first stop, a trailer park on the way out of town toward the "country." Our farm was a full five miles from school, but suburbia touched the land most of the way. Back when my father was growing up, the city of Minneapolis might have seemed like a continent away, but now it was connected without a single gap to the vast suburban area surrounding the city.

My stop was nearly the last. After twenty minutes of riding the bumpy, smelly bus, Tracy said, "Where on earth do you live, anyway?"

"It's not much farther now," I said, trying not to be defensive or embarrassed. "That farm over there, see the silo? That's my uncle's place. And the one way over there — one of my great-uncle's. My dad's family settled here three generations ago. They came from Czechoslovakia and divided up the land into several farms. My dad's is one of the biggest. His grandfather must have been some kind of leader. This place has quite a history."

My companions looked impressed, but I wondered if I was talking too much.

"Are all those yours by any chance?" Rachel pointed to our large pumpkin patch. The bus halted at last.

"Yes, they're nearly ready to pick too. You'll have to come out here again soon." We stepped off the bus, and I gestured toward one side of our large yard. "My dad always piles them up near the driveway, for easy loading. He makes this great orange, lumpy mountain of pumpkins. When I was little, he would let me climb it, but, of course, once I got big enough to smush them, that had to stop."

As we got off the bus, I noticed that Tracy and Rachel were looking at me, and I couldn't quite tell if they were curious, surprised, just interested, or maybe even a little envious.

Tracy glanced around and tugged on her long blond ponytail. She seemed a little preoccupied, and I wondered why the two of them had to pick this particular day to have a fight.

Rachel was giving me a very friendly smile. "Where did you say your dad piled the pumpkins? Over there?"

I smiled back, grateful for her interest. "Yes. I used to think that he piled them just for me. So I could see them when I got off the school bus every day and see how much bigger the mountain was than the day before. Isn't that dumb? And then Mom would sometimes . . ."

To my dismay, tears choked off the rest of my words.

I shook my head and led the way to my house. "Sorry about that. I've been . . ." Why, I wondered, had I set myself up for this? What were these girls doing here, anyway? Maybe being alone wasn't so bad.

Rachel wrapped her arm around me as we walked. "It kind of sneaks up on you, huh?" she said. "At the most unexpected times? When my grandpa died a couple of years ago, I didn't think I'd ever get over it."

I looked at her, surprised. She did seem to understand.

"Nice house," Rachel continued. "It looks so . . . welcoming."

"Thanks," I said. I stared discreetly at her face for a moment. Although she was a bit overweight, I thought Rachel had an unusual beauty, with her shoulder-length, blunt-cut hair and dark, quick eyes. Her features all seemed exactly right for her face, as though designed by an artist attentive to details — the projection of each bone, the contrast of flushed cheeks to straight ivory forehead. This, I decided, was a face I could be comfortable with. Especially since its owner was so apparently unaware of its beauty.

"Is your dad home?" Tracy eyed Rachel's arm around me. "I hope we aren't going to be any bother."

"He's probably working. He'll be in soon."

We settled into my room upstairs. I'd cleaned it so thoroughly for the occasion that I hardly recognized it. But it was soon comfortably cluttered again. There was barely room to walk once sleeping bags and suitcases started spilling open and spreading out.

80

When Tracy pulled a handful of papers out of her suitcase, she glanced at Rachel and then at me, then stuck them under her nightgown.

Rachel watched this with a curious gleam in her eye. "I knew it. That's what you were getting at, isn't it? What are they? Leaflets for us to distribute, Mandy and I? Maybe some Xeroxed articles we just *have* to read or else we should be ashamed of ourselves?"

"Drop it, Rachel," Tracy said.

I looked at the two of them, bewildered.

"Mandy," Rachel said with exaggerated courtesy, "allow me to introduce you to the 'new' Tracy Anderson, budding activist. Going to Berkeley — "

"Sh-sh-sh," Tracy stopped her. "I think I heard Mandy's dad come in." She left the room.

I smiled nervously at Rachel. "What's the — "

"Later." She helped me up off the floor.

". . . Stacy?" Dad was asking when we joined them downstairs.

"Tracy," I corrected. "And this is Rachel."

"You'll be tested after supper," Rachel said. "I'm the chubby one." Her face was still red from what had started upstairs; she looked ready to fight, contemptuous of polite small talk. She began to explore our dining room by herself.

Tracy, however, chatted coolly, almost flirtatiously, with Dad. "It must be lovely having this place," Tracy said. "Mandy explained to us on the way out here how long it's been in your family, Mr. Smetana."

"Yes, it is . . . has," Dad said. He was inching over

81

to stand by me. For a moment I thought he might end up behind me.

"It's getting rare these days for anyone to value land, don't you think?" Tracy went on. "I mean, the government is much more interested in other people's land, other countries, don't you think?"

Dad mumbled cautious agreement, but it seemed to me that he suddenly veered away from the conversation, that he wanted to get away from us without being rude.

"We're making pizza tonight, Dad," I said. "It might take us a while, so why don't you go ahead and relax in your chair? We'll call you when it's ready."

Tracy took charge in the kitchen, since she was the only one who had ever made pizza from scratch. I was second in command since I knew where everything was and since I had bought the ingredients she had ordered.

Once in the kitchen for a while, I became painfully aware of how it must have looked to the others — such a plain, functional, overused room. It had always seemed much cheerier to me before. Now there I was with these girls I hardly knew, opening cupboards, moving things around, trying to have fun.

"No, no, Rachel," Tracy said at one point. "Knead the dough; don't punch it. Knead it."

Rachel clutched her dough with floury hands, pressed it to her cheek and said, "Dough — I knead you!"

With that, Tracy gave her best friend's shoulder a little squeeze, and I was relieved that they had apparently made up.

A little later Rachel grabbed the pepperoni, ready to

slice it, but held it in her hand instead, staring at it obscenely. Tracy and I glanced at her and started to giggle.

"What's the matter with you two?" Rachel stroked the pepperoni with her fingers suggestively. "My gosh," she said. "I think it's growing!"

At this I doubled over with laughter, perhaps overdoing it, but I felt good. Tracy-the-commander tried to restore order. "Rachel, cut it out. Mandy's dad could come in here any minute."

Rachel shrugged, winked at me and started slicing the pepperoni.

Somehow we managed to stick two presentable pizzas into the oven, set the table and wait, chatting about school. I called Dad when we took the pizzas out later to fill the kitchen with their spicy scent.

He sniffed and said, "Smells good." When he had been served a slice, he added, "Good. Pepperoni — my favorite." He looked bewildered and a little hurt when we howled at his comment, but otherwise the meal was a success.

*

We were sitting in our nightgowns on the floor of my room. Tracy blinked out her contact lenses, put on some granny glasses and pulled out a pack of cigarettes. "Want one?"

"No thanks," I said, unsure if that was the correct answer.

Rachel gave me a motherly nod. "Thatta girl. Tracy thinks she looks sophisticated when she smokes."

I had noticed all evening how often things were explained to me, and I was getting tired of it.

Tracy lifted a pair of blue jeans out of her suitcase. "See what I've been doing to these old things?"

"Embroidery," Rachel said as she peered at them. "Real pretty, Trace. You're looking more like a hippie every day."

"I'm not trying to look like anything. I'm just expressing my individuality —"

"By dressing like all the other 'flower children'?"

"Well, better that than like the rest of the kids around here. Honestly, I wish our school weren't so darn backward. That stupid dress code, which just about every other school in the world has abolished. And hassling everybody about their long hair . . ."

I tried to conjure up a picture of how everybody dressed in our school, surprised that it was even an issue. Then I realized that most of us didn't really match at all the image of kids that the newspapers and magazines presented. Why hadn't it occurred to me before?

"What are you scowling about, Mandy?" Rachel asked. "You seem off in another world."

"Sometimes I think I am."

Rachel gazed at me, clearly waiting for more. Her face was scrubbed, and I decided I liked it even better without makeup.

I glanced at Tracy, embarrassed at what I was about to admit. "I guess I'm just not very involved in what's going on today. I mean, I read and watch the news and sense that really enormous changes have been taking place in the last couple of years, but somehow that doesn't make *me* feel a part of it."

I thought Tracy looked a little disgusted, but also that she was fighting the impulse to put me down. She shrugged and tapped ashes from her cigarette into the cup she was using as an ashtray. Her hair hung down almost to her waist, straight as paper except for the kink in it where the rubber band had been.

"I think that's pretty understandable," Rachel said, "with all that's happened to you lately. Your mom and stuff. I even heard you and what's-his-name broke up."

I nodded.

"Maybe this is a private matter," Tracy said. She seemed impatient, perhaps bored.

Rachel glared at her. "It's a pretty important matter — important to some people." She turned to me. "When did it happen? I want to hear it all."

"Last weekend." I searched for some graceful way out of this conversation, but I had no idea what to replace it with. I knew Rachel was just being concerned and, maybe with her alone, as warm as she was, I could have talked about Peter. But Tracy looked so uncomfortable. "We just had a fight, that's all."

"Was it about sex?" Tracy watched the glowing end of her cigarette.

I stared at her for a moment. "What makes you ask that?"

"I know about these things."

Rachel snorted and shoved Tracy out of our triangle.

"I do," Tracy insisted. Her hair had spread around

her shoulders now like a cape. "What else would it be?"

"Plenty of things," Rachel answered. After watching me for a while, apparently gauging my mood and finding it too somber, she said, "Hey, somebody ask me if I smoke after sex."

"No," Tracy groaned, "don't. That's the grossest joke. Besides, everybody's heard it already."

I didn't volunteer the information that I had not.

"Oops, sorry," Rachel said. "There I go again, being superficial and . . . what was that other word you used today? *Flip?* Yes, that was it." She started brushing her hair almost savagely. My scalp stung watching her. "Not concerned enough about Vietnam and such."

"Would you mind dropping all this?" Tracy asked. "I'm sure Mandy didn't invite us over here to watch us fight."

I moved almost imperceptibly and looked out the window at the moonless night. Alone. It was as if I'd walked in on something, in the middle. The intruder, the misfit. There was too much catching up to do.

Rachel drew me back in. "Mandy, did you know that Tracy changed her plans, *our* plans, for Vassar next year? She's going to Berkeley, because, she says, that's where it's all happening, whatever 'it' is."

"Berkeley's a good school," I offered. "I got their catalogue." This sounded so lame, I didn't blame Tracy for ignoring it. I turned back toward my window.

"How on earth," Tracy asked, "can we have lived through a year like last year and not be changed, *radically* changed?"

She was addressing Rachel, but I felt my face burn.

86

"I mean, Martin Luther King's and Bobby Kennedy's murders, and the Chicago convention, all that horrible violence. And the war news every day . . . it makes me . . . physically sick. It really does. I can't help it." She had indeed gotten quite pale in the last few seconds, and her eyes brimmed with tears.

Rachel tugged gently on Tracy's nightgown, a gesture that struck me as one of profound sadness. "Oh, Trace. You used to be — We used to be . . . I don't know. All these years we've been so close and now . . . you're so . . . different." Rachel looked to me for understanding, but I didn't know how to give it.

Tracy watched Rachel's fingers, which were still tugging. Then she tugged back. "People have to change sometimes," she said quietly.

Rachel let go of Tracy's nightgown and examined her hands as if for traces of the flannel left on them. Then she straightened her back and raked at the sides of her hair with all ten fingers. The gesture reminded me of Peter.

Tracy looked at me and cleared her throat. "Maybe we should get back to talking about sex."

Rachel gave me an embarrassed smile. "Maybe we should. Sex is always good for laughs."

Tracy and I laughed obediently.

"So . . ." we all three said at once and then laughed again. A silence settled on us like snow. If Lynn were here, I told myself, there would be none of these silences.

I felt obliged to say something. Anything would do.

"Peter," I blurted out, realizing that his name had been on my mind most of the evening, "was . . . sure a . . . great kisser."

Rachel shrieked, and Tracy shook her head in disbelief.

"Hey, that's right," Rachel said. "He's a trumpet player, isn't he? Well-developed lips."

We all giggled and I felt looser, more ready to talk. "I don't have any idea why I said that. It just sort of . . . well, this is the first . . . no, second, Friday night in ages I haven't been out with him, you know. I feel . . ." I wanted to say *lonely*, but I thought that might offend them. "Lost."

Rachel wrapped her arms tightly around her knees. She looked more serious again. The laugh lines at the corners of her mouth were not twitching at all. I decided she was full of surprises.

Tracy started to say something and then changed her mind. I figured it would have been something like "You're better off without him."

I felt my face flush again; I longed for my cool, dark window. But no, I had to keep trying. "I'm afraid I'm not very good at this," I said, almost to myself.

"At what?" Rachel asked.

"Talking. To girl friends, that is. Peter was really a very good friend." I swallowed. "Here I've got all these feelings inside me — about my mom, about just about everything — and I just wish I could . . . oh, I don't know." Belong, I thought. Like I used to belong with him.

"Give yourself some time," Rachel suggested.

"That's right," Tracy said. "In the meantime, how about some laughs? Rachel here knows thousands of dirty jokes. Isn't it about time for those . . . and popcorn?"

"Popcorn, yes." I breathed deeply. "And dirty jokes. What a great idea."

"No sweat," Rachel said. "How dirty do you want them?"

"She has this elaborate system of categorization," Tracy said, "based on groans, moans, shivers, shudders and . . . what's the last one?"

"Strangulation of the joke-teller."

"Oh, yes. That's right. But first, the popcorn."

We tiptoed downstairs, suddenly aware of how late it was. We continued to tiptoe and whisper until we returned to my room even though the corn popping could surely have awakened Dad anyway.

We sat back down in my room, in a smaller triangle than before. Rachel's left knee touched my right one. "And now," she said, "to begin."

I looked at her, wondering if she had only meant the joke-telling, and I could tell she had not. I sensed we were beginning something much more important and had a sudden insight. Perhaps it was friendship that I'd been searching for hardest of all.

9

DURING THE NEXT several weeks I found myself
still looking out for Peter's car. Everywhere. Once
I spotted it in town when I was grocery shopping, but it
was two blocks away and headed in the opposite direction. It seemed to me that there was someone in the car
with him, but I wasn't sure.

A friend of his told me Peter had moved into an
apartment shortly after we broke up. I wondered where
it was — how strange not to know where he was living.
I got itchy and almost called him several times, but always hung up before dialing the last digit of his parents'
number. It would be difficult asking his mom or dad for
his new phone number. Not knowing what he'd told
them about us, I wasn't sure how to deal with them.
They'd always liked me, I knew, but were reserved about
it . . . especially his mom.

I saw a lot of Rachel and Tracy, but mostly at school.
Lynn was still acting very cool toward me. She seemed

uncomfortable, even embarrassed, around me, and I couldn't imagine how she could still be mad about something so silly.

Weekends loomed larger than before, harder to fill. I slept more than usual, ate less. Then everyone started talking about Homecoming and I knew that was why I had almost called Peter. We had rarely missed a major school dance together, and now I was about to miss one of my last before graduating.

In mid-October, on the Friday two weeks before Homecoming, Rachel and I got together. Tracy had gone to some kind of meeting or peace rally, and Rachel was anxious to have fun without her. I didn't feel badly about being "used" in this way because I was doing pretty much the same thing with Rachel.

We went to see a movie, *Goodbye Columbus*, which depressed me because it made me think of Peter so much. I hated myself for identifying with Brenda Patimkin, a spoiled, immature girl who misplaced her boyfriend's love as easily, it seemed, as the contraceptive device she had purchased for their intimacy. Leaving the diaphragm for her horrified mother to find, Brenda made it easier on herself: of course, she could never see Neil again. Her parents said so.

I cried so hard at the end that Rachel stayed with me in our seats while most of the audience left. She didn't try to say anything, but she was there next to me where I couldn't bear an empty space right then.

We were still seated when the audience for the next feature began to file in. As I was stuffing wet Kleenex into my purse and getting ready to leave, I heard a faint gasp from Rachel.

"What's the matter?" I asked.

She shook her head. "Nothing. Let's go." She gestured toward the farther exit.

"What is — ?" But then I saw them, walking down the aisle and finding seats a few rows ahead and to the left of us — Peter and Lynn. He was gesturing with his left hand for her to sit down and she was smoothing her skirt, acting shy. He was wearing a wine-colored cardigan sweater I had never seen. I looked away. Closing my eyes, I felt a sticky kind of darkness close in on me until Rachel ushered me out of there, off to our right.

"I'm pretty sure they didn't see us," she whispered in the lobby.

Darkness was still after me. I wanted to go to sleep, right then and there. I didn't care much about anything else.

"I can't believe it." Rachel sounded angry and hurt enough for the both of us. "She sure didn't waste any time, did she?"

"Huh?" I tried to focus on what she was saying.

"I heard her talking to Shelley the other day in the bathroom. She's been nuts about Peter forever. 'Now's my chance,' I heard her say."

"Lynn said that? I didn't know she felt that way." Blinking a few times, I wondered aloud, "Maybe she called *him*, then."

Rachel looked at me, her head tilted sideways. "Probably. Hey, do you want to go somewhere else, or should

I take you home? I'm up for a Coke or something. . . ."

"I think I'll go home now."

She put me into her Volkswagen and fastened me into my seat belt as though I were a child. I saw, belatedly, the way Peter's hand had rested on Lynn's back as they had walked leisurely down the aisle. The cuff of his new sweater was rolled up and his hand looked white against her dark shirt. It had a look of belonging there.

"Sure you don't want a Coke?" Rachel said. "Or maybe ice cream? My treat."

"No, thanks." Would *they*, I wondered, go somewhere after the movie? Would Peter think of me at the end when he watched Brenda on the screen, carelessly spoiling a love affair?

Maybe, I thought as Rachel drove me home, maybe they would discuss me, Peter and Lynn. Compare notes. Tear me to shreds. Comfort each other. They'd find all sorts of ways to comfort each other.

*

The next morning, the phone woke me up. It was late, I could tell, but I wanted to find sleep again.

"Phone for you," Dad called upstairs.

I woke up quickly and rushed to the phone, automatically expecting it to be Peter even though that made no sense at all.

It was Rachel. "Hi. Listen, I need to talk to you about this party I'm invited to tonight."

Oh, great, I thought, leaning against the wall and sliding down it into a heap. Just what I need to hear.

"Mandy? You there?"

"Yeah," I said.

"Well, I have this extra invitation — they want another bod, preferably female."

"No, thanks."

"Really. It's going to be fun. It's at a friend of mine's house who goes to the Academy. I mentioned Mark before, didn't I? You know, the guys he bums around with are superbright and —"

"Thanks for thinking of me, really. But you ought to see me right now. I'm a sight. They'd probably ask to see my ID as a human being." I noticed that talking to Rachel made me joke around even when I felt that laughter might have dried up forever.

"Hey, I can help you there. I'm a miracle worker when it comes to bad moods and what they do to the human face. I can get you looking *better* than human. No sweat."

"Well, I don't know. Maybe next time." I knew I had no right to feel so hurt. Peter and I had, after all, broken up. And as for Lynn, her avoiding me had had nothing to do with any mistreatment from me. She was embarrassed, that's all. It didn't bother or surprise me that she had chosen Peter over me.

"Mandy, you need some fun. I can tell. How about if I come to pick you up at four and you can get ready over here? It'll be great."

*

Rachel was right, at least about getting me to look better. She was masterful with makeup, which seemed to reassure and comfort her even though she needed it less

94

than I did. Before I knew it, my eyes were almost sparkling, my unremarkable cheekbones highlighted elegantly ("I've had lots of practice with cheeks," she informed me, puffing hers out like a blowfish.), and my hair was retrained into a fresher, wispier style.

"Ta Da!" Rachel said proudly as we admired me in the mirror. Then, "Yikes, look at me! I've only got two hours to fix this." She mugged at me in the mirror, and I felt so much better I wanted to hug her. "Thanks," I said.

"It was nothing. You've got natural good looks — I just helped them along."

"No, I mean for inviting me. For insisting. For making me laugh." Rachel struck me then as one of the strongest people I had ever met. This is what I want to be like, I thought. Exactly.

"No sweat. Now you can help me."

"How?"

"I need to lose fifteen pounds in two hours."

I laughed again.

"Say, it's easy to make you laugh. Easier than I expected. Old Tracy's the one who suggested I invite you, to cheer you up or something. I think she's sort of throwing us together, don't you? Maybe because I'm a very demanding friend to have and she's too busy these days. Too committed, you know?"

I nodded. The thought of Tracy "throwing us together" fascinated me, especially since I wasn't in the least bit hurt or surprised that Tracy didn't appear to "want" me for herself. She must consider me "backward," like our school, I thought. And self-centered. But Rachel didn't seem to mind that about me; it really did appear that she and I should become good friends.

We finished getting ready together at a leisurely pace. Rachel examined what I had brought to wear before choosing what she would put on. I appreciated her insurance against my being an oddball. To me a party meant wearing a dress and heels, but I recalled Tracy's disgust with dress codes and my own apparent blindness to style. I vowed to go shopping for some new, trendier clothes soon.

The party took place only a few houses down the hilly road from Rachel's. The clacking sound our shoes made echoed in the silent, smoky air of the neighborhood. "A lot of fireplaces around here," I said.

"Are you kidding? I have a friend who has one in her bathroom. Can you imagine? Very status-y. Pretentious. Makes me kind of sick, if you want the truth. I'm anxious to get out of here next year."

"Why? I'd love to live in one of these houses, even for just a week."

"Really?" Her eyes narrowed as she surveyed the street. "Maybe I'll try to straighten you out sometime, but right now, we're here."

The door opened into a two-story foyer. Large glass bulbs of light were suspended far above us, and under our feet, there was pale gray shag carpeting. The size and austerity of the living room made me feel small and about to break something. My red knit dress, which had always made me feel so chic, clashed harshly with the mauve furnishings.

I tried to attend to all the introductions, but the only names I knew for sure were Rachel's, her friend Mark's and mine, although even mine seemed open to debate. Rachel leaned over to whisper to me as I stared at my feet, unsteady on the plush shag. "This carpeting is something, isn't it?" she said. "Don't take off your shoes; they'd have to send in a search party."

I giggled. Clinging to a plastic cup of punch and chewing off my lipstick, I studied the other guests. What an odd mixture of people, I thought. Mark and several others were dressed conservatively, exactly as I had pictured guys from a prestigious private school to look. I felt comfortable enough with them since I had dressed up similarly. But, sprinkled throughout the room were colorful tunics, tie-dyed shirts, frayed bell-bottom jeans that dragged on the floor, peasant-style blouses and skirts, and, of course, beads.

There were a few black guys, but no black girls. In one corner some kids were smoking something rather suspicious until Mark approached and said something to them. In another corner sat a young man picking out tunes on his guitar and murmuring lyrics. Nobody paid much attention to him.

Nearby I could hear a group discussing President Nixon and his "absurd lack of perspective" on the Vietnam War. "He doesn't hear us, or see us," one guy was saying. "He doesn't even try. When I was there in Washington last year, at the peace rally, I caught a glimpse of him. The SOB looks like he's made of wax." It struck me as amazing that the war was being talked about so energetically, without fear of spoiling everyone's evening. You must get used to it, I decided, this talking about the unspeakable. Maybe, eventually, you start losing your sense of powerlessness.

Blending with the talk of war and peace, and with the music from a rock radio station, there were discussions about colleges. I recalled, with some regret, that Rachel would be leaving for Vassar next year. I watched the way her dark eyes followed the action in the room, gobbling stray words as though they all formed a neat trail. Occasionally she raked at the sides of her hair (a gesture of hers that never seemed to wreck her hairdo) and then tugged at the fabric straining around her hips. When she caught my eye, she flipped me double peace signs and made a mocking, jowl-shaking Nixon-face. Why, I asked myself, couldn't we have become friends much sooner?

Soon she plumped herself down next to me with a heaping plate of snacks, which she offered to share with me. "Having fun? Isn't Tricky Dick *your* favorite topic of conversation? Seriously, don't let all this talk put you off. Pretty soon the dancing and necking will start, just like at any old party you've been to. You'll feel more at home."

I looked at her with a frown.

"Geez, did *that* come out wrong. See? I'm nervous too. Come on, eat this stuff or I will."

"Rachel, I feel out of it here. You know, the old farm-girl thing." I wondered how she could possibly know what I meant, but I trusted her to try.

"Hey, haven't you noticed all the guys giving you the once-over? Some farm girl. Huh! Don't be such a snob."

She looked up at someone standing behind me. "Hi, Gary. Have you met my friend Mandy? She's embarrassed because she lives so much better than Mark and I do."

"Rachel!" I didn't look up at Gary yet, feeling my face go red-hot.

"Well, you do. You've got a whole farm to call your own. What've we got but a few oak trees apiece and houses so soundproof you can't hear yourself sneeze? Big deal."

I turned to Gary then as he sat down on the other side of me. He was black and I found myself, for a moment, more surprised by him than I wanted to be.

"Farm, eh?" he said. "What kind of farm?" He was tall, a bit too slender, and looked about my age but somehow seemed more dignified about it. Maybe it was the tweed jacket.

"Truck farm," I answered. "Berries, tomatoes, stuff like that. About five miles south of town."

"I used to fantasize about living on a farm," he said. "I've always lived in town, in a little house that looks just like all the others around it. Must be great to have space, huh?"

I hoped my face was toning down by that time.

"Do you have any horses?"

I laughed, beginning to relax a little. "No, it probably isn't the kind of place you fantasized about. We did have an old nag named Queenie for years, though. I used to ride her around the yard when I was four and feed her rotten apples from my palms. Does that count?"

"Sure. I've only been on a horse once myself, but it

was great." Gary's smile was on the shy side, but his eyes had a depth and warmth to them that made him look as much at ease as he made me feel.

"Do you go to the Academy with Mark?" I discreetly examined his hair, which was styled in a medium-length Afro. I wanted to touch it for some reason, never having been so close to hair like that. Since there were no blacks in our school, I realized I'd never actually talked to anyone like Gary before.

"Yeah. Mark's a good friend of mine. Some house he's got, though, huh? Never have quite gotten over it."

Rachel had drifted away from us and I didn't see her again until later when the records started and she caught my eye while dancing with Mark.

Gary and I spent the rest of the evening together, mostly dancing, sometimes talking. When Gary first asked me to dance, I hesitated. Would the others think it was odd? Looking around the room for clues and finding none, I simply put myself in his very capable hands. And I was glad I did.

The party, for some reason, was not well supplied with records, a slipup that I would have thought impossible at such a gathering. The best record they had was an old favorite, Simon and Garfunkel's *Sounds of Silence*, and Gary and I must have danced to that a half-dozen times.

He held me with a reserved kind of interest. If it bothered him that I was white, he didn't show it. I figured he must have danced with white girls often, since there were so few black families nearby.

Nothing passionate seemed to be happening between

us, but by the middle of the evening we were friends. His seriousness brought out my more frivolous side and I enjoyed making him laugh. I used Rachel's search-party line about the carpeting, adopting it as my own, and he laughed appreciatively.

But at one point, sitting huddled in a corner, we spoke urgently about our futures.

"Teaching, maybe at the college level," he said. "It's what I've always wanted. Nothing more or less. That is, I'm not much of an activist. Self-centered, my mom calls me."

"She doesn't want you to be a teacher?" I asked. "That's hardly a self-centered profession."

"It's not that. It's that she wants me to serve my people more actively, you know? Maybe politically. She keeps hammering at me that in my private school I've got it soft. I'm treated so well because I'm 'one of the smart ones' who supposedly rises above my race. Right? 'Just wait,' she says, 'until you get into the reality outside that school.' "

A couple drifted by us looking fresh from Woodstock. Gary smiled as he watched them. "Even the way I dress bugs her," he said. "It's so funny, like all the other parents in this country are screaming at their kids about their hippie clothes and hair, while my mom thinks I look too establishment." He patted his hair. "I'm growing this out to appease her."

"Your mom sounds . . . well, like a mother, I guess." What a dumb thing to say, I thought to myself. "You don't seem self-centered to me."

Gary looked at me with a spark of anger, and I couldn't

tell where it was aimed. I didn't know if I had said something wrong, or if he was just frustrated in general about being misunderstood.

I tried again. "Can't you serve your people by being a good teacher?"

"I'd like to think so." He looked down at his clenched hands and then slowly seemed to relax them.

I watched him closely and realized, not just that he was black, but that it mattered. It made our experiences so fundamentally different, separate. I wanted very much to close the distance that was creating itself between the two of us before we had even gotten to know each other.

"I guess there are plenty of people who don't want to do what's expected of them." I searched further for the right words. "Maybe activism, for you, is expected in the same way that . . . that I'm expected to get married and have kids."

He smiled a knowing smile.

"Here I am," I continued, "working so hard to get good grades and figure out what, exactly, I'm good at, what I'm meant to do — like you're meant to be a teacher. But then, I'll have to set aside all that for later, right? If I do what's expected."

Gary's eyes were steady. He seemed to be listening to me very carefully. "You're expected to do for other people, not for yourself, for years. And then, maybe, maybe, you can pick up where you left off, huh?"

I nodded.

His hands moved from his gray flannel-clad knees to take my hands and press them together between his. His

102

skin was a rich maple color, but the color in his palms was about the same as mine.

The simple guitar riff began again. The fine, plaintive voices: *Hello darkness, my old friend. I've come to talk with you again.* We danced once more to that song. Oh, my gosh, I thought, giddy from the talk, from the laughter, from the way he looked at me. We've got a song. This is our song! How corny can you get?

It must have been late. Rachel watched impatiently as we danced and gestured at me with my coat. "Let's go," she mouthed.

People talking without speaking. People hearing without listening, answered the voices from the record player.

Gary held me tighter for a moment before letting me go. "I'll call you," he said.

I realized I'd been wanting to hear those words, but when I did, some of the uneasiness from earlier in the evening returned. Was I about to start a relationship with this guy? Why on earth not? I answered myself.

I joined Rachel at the door. My coat collar was warm from her hands; in fact, I felt warm all over. We rushed back to her house. "Rachel. He's nice, isn't he? I mean, do you know him well? Tell me. Tell me everything about him."

"Uh oh," Rachel said. "You're smitten, aren't you? Now don't misunderstand me. Lord knows, I'm not in the least bit prejudiced myself and the times they are a-changing and all that, but what about your dad? How will he feel about your getting interested in a black guy?"

Again the fact of Gary's separateness from me hit hard.

I hadn't even considered Dad's reaction until Rachel brought it up. "Well, I suppose he'll be a typical father about the whole thing. But that doesn't matter anymore, because . . . well, because I'm not really much of a typical daughter these days. Besides, I'm not going to marry the guy. What's the big deal?"

Rachel gave me a look that might have said, "Are you kidding?" Then she said, "Looks like maybe you'll be able to forget old Peter now, eh? That's something."

I wished she hadn't said that. Until then, the evening had been perfect.

10 ~

MANDY," DAD SAID at breakfast the following Friday. "I'll be out tonight. The card club's finally talked me into rejoining as a . . . as a single. There are a few others . . . like me."

"That's great. I'm sure you'll have fun. You need it."

I was glad for him, but I was also relieved that he would be gone. I was going out with Gary and it seemed best to postpone Dad's introduction to him until later. What could Dad say, faced with the fact that Gary and I had already started dating? I had no idea.

"I've got a date," I said, "but I'll probably be home before you. It's just for dinner."

"Well, it's about time — I haven't seen Peter around here for ages."

I didn't correct him. Maybe he figured nobody else would want to ask me out.

Dad soaked up his egg yolk with the last of his toast, finished his coffee and was gone before I could begin to feel guilty. I reassured myself that, after all, Dad and I were trying to live pretty independently of each other now. He was probably hiding things from me too. For all I knew, one of those other "singles" he mentioned might be some widow who was after Dad. He might come up to me someday soon and say, "You're going to have a stepmother, like it or not."

All the way to school I practiced to myself how I could invite Gary to the Homecoming dance when I was with him that night. I was a little nervous because he seemed somehow above the nonsense of school dances. Maybe he'll say no, I thought in panic. I'd better wait for the right moment. "There's this silly dance next weekend," I would say indifferently. "I don't suppose you'd like to go. The band will be awful. And there are always these jerks who end up drunk and try to break the balloons between their thighs and dumb stuff like that. Maybe you'd rather not." Yes, that would make me sound above it all too.

Rachel had already asked Mark and suggested we might double. She was counting on me since Tracy had decided Homecoming was "irrelevant." "Lots of schools," she claimed, "have abolished them. No one cares." I couldn't help but care. I knew next Friday night would be pure hell if I had to stay at home.

Lynn was standing at my locker when I got there, waiting for me. We hadn't spoken more than a few polite words for weeks. "Hey," she said. Her summer freckles, I noticed, were already gone. She looked sheepish, dreadfully guilty.

"Hi, Lynn." My voice was bright, automatically determined to help her out. "How are you these days?"

"Fine. Great." She fidgeted with the collar of her sweater and then dropped half her books.

"What's the matter?" I asked.

"I was wondering . . . if you — I mean, is it okay if I ask . . . Peter to Homecoming?" She exhaled noisily. "I don't know if you know . . . that is — "

"Relax, Lynn. I know you've been dating him."

"You do? Oh, well, I just didn't want you hearing about it from someone after the dance."

"I'll be there too." I bit the inside of my cheek.

"You will? Great. With who?"

"You don't know him. He goes to the Academy."

"Oh." Some of the color returned to her face. She stared at her fingernails, which appeared to be freshly polished. I had always envied Lynn her perfect, oval nails. They looked as if they belonged in a magazine ad. Mine never seemed to outgrow, from one summer to the next, the effects of tying and pruning tomato plants.

I couldn't stand her silence another second. "So, I guess I'll see you there." My heart was pounding harder because I realized I would, if I went to the dance, see her there with Peter.

"I'm sorry, Mandy. I know it's awkward. But you did dump him, and you know how I've always felt about him."

"No, not really," I managed to say. I was beginning to feel a bit sick to my stomach. Had Peter really told her I'd *dumped* him?

"You did too know how I felt about him. I never tried

107

to hide anything from you. Never." She rushed off toward the band room.

I leaned my forehead against the cool metal of my locker. If I closed my eyes and concentrated hard, I could still feel Peter's lips surprising the back of my neck, raising the little hairs there. His hands would circle me slowly to meet at my front, rest a moment as if weary from the journey, and then begin his fingertip trace of the invisible, sensitive line running vertically from my breastbone downward. My breathing would gradually catch up with his, my back against his chest, seemingly connected.

The bell sounded and brought me crashing back to the reality of my cold locker. "Damn you, Lynn," I whispered into the hard metallic emptiness. I figured she knew his magic already. Damn her! I swore, if Gary turned me down, I'd call Peter and ask him to forgive me enough to go to the dance with me. I would make him choose. And what were a few weeks of dates with Lynn and good-night kisses compared to what he and I had had together? I slammed the locker shut and ran to band.

*

That night I took a leisurely bath after Dad had finished in the bathroom. His meeting started at 7:00 and Gary was picking me up at 7:15.

"Dinner," he had said on the phone. "At Chez Antoine."

"Chez Antoine! That's quite a posh restaurant. Sounds great."

After hanging up, I had repeated the word *posh* to myself. Such a strange word for me to use — a favorite of my mom's for a while. Her "posh period," I had affectionately dubbed it. It had been several years ago, one of her many flights of fancy.

She and Dad had gone to an English movie, one of those that Dad claimed should be supplied with subtitles. But afterward everything was "posh" for a while, from the new couch to a late Saturday evening dinner that none of us had adequately appreciated. My brother Greg, in fact, had shown the bad taste to get diarrhea from it. But Mom only sipped her costly wine (the price sticker ripped off before Dad could see it) and gazed into the light from the stub of a candle.

When she had brought home a large pink box one day, however, and unwrapped from the pink floral tissue paper her new "posh frock," Dad had shouted at her, "You're carrying this too far. Way too far. Farmers' wives don't wear *posh frocks*."

"*This* one does," Mom had answered, cool as could be.

Now, after my bath, smiling at the memory and facing my closet, I searched for a posh-enough frock for Gary and Chez Antoine. Mom would have relished the challenge. "Let's see," she might say. "How about this cute lilac one?"

"*Too* cute," I answered. "Not sophisticated enough." From the very back of my closet, I produced a gray wool sheath. "Now this is sophisticated." But upon closer examination, I remembered why I never wore it — it itched.

I imagined Mom rooting through my closet over and over as if a miraculous, forgotten "frock" might spring from it to be proclaimed perfect.

"It's hopeless, Mom. I'm still the farm girl playing dress-up." I pulled out an old floral number that was much too springy but had always inspired compliments.

Seated at the mirror, I tried to copy what Rachel had done to my hair and face. But my hair presented me with a brand-new cowlick just above my right ear. I tried hair spray, which only made it sticky. Maybe, I thought, I could favor my left side. But there, on my left cheek, had sprouted a blemish — a large, angry pomegranate-seed of a pimple. I wondered if Gary would mind if I sat with my back to him.

When Gary arrived, he asked, first thing, where my Dad was.

"He's playing cards. He'll be late." As an afterthought, I added, "He was sorry he couldn't meet you."

"Next time," Gary said with his shiest, most charming smile. My hopes for Homecoming soared.

"You look very nice," he told me, but he sounded as though he were merely being polite. I wanted to assure him that, when I was at my best, I was really quite attractive.

"How's school going?" I asked later at the restaurant, longing desperately to somehow recapture that "Sounds of Silence" atmosphere of the party. "Did you get that independent study you wanted? About the civil rights movement's influence on American literature?"

He shook his head. "No. But I've got the proposal in

shape, at least." He had been looking around us since we'd entered the building. I found myself doing the same and I knew instinctively what we were watching for — the stray, hate-filled glance, the whispered comment, some indication that our presence together, black and white, was going to be challenged. Why hadn't I anticipated this?

I wondered what we would do if we *were* challenged. Gary had indicated a sort of passive resistance as his way of dealing with discrimination. Maybe, I thought in horror, I would have to be the one to deal with it, to snarl out some defense against racism in this dim, tasteful place. Maybe I was doing something rather daring without even knowing it.

It became clear, very quickly, however, that this French restaurant was not The World and any anticipation of trouble seemed to disperse with the barely audible, piped-in hum of violins. I tried to relax.

We discussed the menu — I chose fish, since it seemed the easiest to eat — and then our stark white, black and chrome surroundings. I almost remarked on the appropriateness of the color scheme, but stopped myself in time.

When the menus were taken from us, we were faced with only each other. "This is such a nice place, Gary. Have you been here before?"

To my delight, he admitted that he had not. I wondered why, then, he seemed to fit in so neatly.

A strained silence descended on us over our French onion soup. The thick cheese would have gummed up our words even if we'd had some to offer. Finally, I said, "Seniors. I just can't believe this is it, can you?"

"Actually, I can. It seems like I've been in school forever. Although . . . I did skip a year along the way."

"You did? You mean you're younger than m——, than the rest of us?"

He frowned into his empty bowl, then looked up at me with an embarrassed smile that I read to mean something like: Why can't I keep my mouth shut? I still felt a little unnerved by this information, though. Since when had I been so immature?

"The only reason I could skip a grade," he said, "is because studying is all I've ever known how to do. I'm sure no athlete, and my social life would barely fill two lines of my journal."

I giggled nervously. He kept a journal, something I had always had difficulty doing. Sometimes, writing things down seemed to trivialize them, and other times it seemed to make more of them than they were worth, and I would end up feeling dishonest. "Dear Diary. Today was the best day of my life so far. I got an A on my English composition and Mr. Johnson told me I would without a doubt win a Pulitzer prize someday (just kidding. Ha ha). Went to the store and saw you-know-who and came home. I hate my hair. Bye for now."

"Mandy?"

"Hm-m-m?"

Gary grinned at me. "You were very far away just then."

"Oh, I was thinking about diaries. How funny they are."

112

"Well, you're lucky you can afford to think of them as funny. My mom sees to it that I take journal writing very seriously. As if I were going to be another Baldwin or Ellison."

Our soup bowls were whisked away and replaced by salad plates.

Gary picked up his fork and gave me a broad, reassuring smile. "Anyway, like I said, I haven't had much to write about, socially at least." After a long, shiver-producing gaze at me, he continued, "Until last weekend, that is. Last Saturday I could've written about meeting someone special, someone altogether refreshing, who told me all about her old horse, Queenie, and who made me laugh and made me think."

I felt myself blushing fiercely and grabbed my goblet of ice water. Several sips later, I felt able to speak again. Except I couldn't think of anything to say. Another silence followed, and then, after the usual remarks about our entrées, still another awkward silence.

I wondered vaguely if we were having this problem because he was black and I was white. I didn't remember worrying about how to talk to him at the party, and I was embarrassed to have even thought of it now. He was new and new people are hard to talk to, that's all. His color had been of mild interest to me for a while, but when we were alone it was easy to forget about it.

Still, I wondered what had gone wrong until I realized that it was more a case of nothing having gone great. Gary's sudden attentiveness had caught me so off guard that we both seemed to back away from each other after that. But wasn't this usually the way on first dates?

113

Of course it was, I reassured myself. An elaborate dance, littered with missteps and breaks in the music.

Maybe if I could see this guy in grubby jeans and an elbowed-out shirt. Peter had uncommonly sharp elbows (or else he simply worked his arms more vigorously than most people) and that was where his shirts always wore out. I'd seen Peter in just about every way imaginable, even asleep a couple of times on our porch after his lunch break from farmwork. And he had seen me every which way too. It was comforting somehow to know that. With Gary, on the other hand, I felt I had to keep myself straightened up, check for smeared mascara or a spot of food at the corner of my mouth.

The fancy restaurant was a mistake for a first date, I decided. In our conversation, we couldn't "kick off our shoes."

Peter had taken me to a similar place on a recent birthday, but that was different — we were both out of place and laughed our way through it. When the waiter had brought a pale scoop of sherbet to each of us between courses, I'd said, "You must have the wrong table. We're not ready for dessert yet."

The waiter had patiently explained that the "sorbet" was intended to "cleanse the palates."

"Oh." I had checked Peter's face, which seemed to say he hadn't known that either, and as soon as the waiter left, freeing us from constraint, we laughed, quietly, until tears plopped into our palate-cleansing sorbet. "How *gauche* of me," I said, and Peter agreed, nose high and lips pursed, "Oh, my, yes. *Très gauche* indeed." The rest of the evening, all one of us had had to do to start giggling again was ask, "Is it time for dessert yet?"

In comparison, my meal with Gary went uneventfully. *Pleasant* was the word that occurred to me. I had the uneasy, if somewhat flattering feeling that he was enjoying himself more than I was.

He told me more about his family, mainly his father, a lawyer who had worked his way out of an urban ghetto by sheer force of will and smarts. The family had moved to Minnesota from Detroit when Gary was seven, and he had been in private schools since he was twelve. He was visibly proud of his father; the shine of his brown eyes intensified when he spoke of him.

Then, as if I'd changed the subject for him, he started talking about his mother. "Of course, she hates it here. She says she misses all her people. Always, she talks about *her people*, as if we're supposed to feel ashamed of our white neighborhood and friends. As if Dad and I have changed in some way, gotten lighter-skinned or something. Can you believe that? After all my dad's work.

"Now that my sisters and I are grown, Mom spends a lot of time back in Detroit. I suppose they're separated, my parents are, but they never call it that. *Divorce* is a bad word to my mom — a white, middle-class epidemic."

I finished eating my fish and drank the rest of my water. I felt sympathy for this woman whom I'd never met, but I didn't dare speak of it. I supposed I was just mother-conscious and maybe a little jealous that Gary still had one whom he didn't appear to appreciate. But there seemed to be something else behind my feelings for this isolated, unhappy woman.

By the time we left the restaurant, we had returned to safer, academic topics of conversation.

"Literature is never going to be the same," Gary said at one point after we'd been driving for a while. "The seventies are going to bring out a whole generation of new minority writers, including women." He glanced at me. "In the last several years, the image of the typical American family that existed in books and taught us how to look at ourselves has been shown to be anything *but* typical. And it was about time."

"It's none of my business," I said, "but it seems to me that you probably agree with your mother, that you're on the same side."

Gary stared at the road ahead. His hands were clenched on the steering wheel. "Of course we're on the same side."

I wished I'd kept my mouth shut. Maybe I'd managed to place myself firmly on the "other side." I knew that was where his mother would see me.

But then I realized that he was not angry at me after all. His hand groped in the dark for mine. "She'd like you."

"Your mother? I doubt, from what you've said, that she'd approve of your dating a white girl."

"She'd be able to see right off that you're special."

At my front door I thanked him for the evening and he kissed me. His lips were smooth and polite, not like Peter's searching, hungry lips. Gary's seemed to want *mine* to be the searching, hungry ones.

116

I decided this was the right moment to ask my question. "Gary, you know that our Homecoming dance is coming up soon, and uh . . . maybe it's not exactly —"

"I'd love to go with you." He sounded as though he had been expecting the invitation. Perhaps he had already talked to Mark. "I'll call you later in the week, okay?"

"Great." I went inside, feeling not quite great. This would be such a different Homecoming that I wondered if I'd have been better off skipping it altogether. Gary kept me off balance, but maybe that was good. And I recalled the kindness and intelligence I saw in his face. I had trouble thinking of him sexually, but that probably had more to do with my recent problems with Peter than anything else.

I raced upstairs and closed my door. Minutes later, Dad came home. I waited for the sound of Dad's bedroom door closing before I made any noise.

"Who are you hiding from?" It was Mom's voice, from somewhere inside me, deeper than usual.

"You know who."

"Your dad?"

"Well, what's he going to say when he meets Gary?" Mom was silent.

"I know I should tell him ahead of time, but maybe he'll say I can't go."

"Maybe," Mom said.

"If you were here . . ."

"What if I were?"

"You could smooth things over. You always did be-

fore. You'd like Gary. You'd say the right things to Dad,
so he wouldn't mind. So he wouldn't be . . . you know,
prejudiced."

I could feel Mom's disapproval.

"Oh, I know. You and Dad were brought up differently from me. But that's just it — *you* would let me go
out with Gary in a minute."

Mom's voice was being unusually elusive. "Mom, talk
to me. I need you."

"Talk to *him.* Talk to your father. Leave me out of it
because that's the way things are now."

I went to sleep with Mom's advice nudging me. *"Talk
to him. Talk to your father."*

II ⟿

W HERE'VE YOU BEEN the last few days?" I asked
Lynn Thursday morning. We were in the instrument room at the same time, which hardly ever
happened anymore.

She looked pale and fidgety. "Around," she said.
"Listen." She drew me into a corner. "I've got to talk to
you today. Can we meet after lunch? At the door by the
playing field?"

"Sure. I'll even eat fast. See you about eleven fifty."

"Thanks, Mandy."

After lunch I barely resisted the urge to stand her up.
The Homecoming dance was the next night and I figured she wanted to talk about that for some reason. What
was the point? There would be some awkwardness for a
few minutes, and that would be that.

Lynn was waiting for me by the door and I couldn't
tell if she was relieved I had come or not. She sighed
several times between our usual comments about school.
Finally she blurted out, "I've just got to talk to you. To
someone. Please. I know it's not right, but you're the
only one I can possibly talk to about this."

We sat down on the dry, scratchy grass at the edge of the playing field.

"About what?" A feeling of dread was beginning to snake its way through me.

She curled herself into a tight ball. "Peter."

I resisted the ridiculous urge to say "Peter who?"

"It's just that, well . . . I've been feeling so — Oh, I can't!" She sprang up and wandered farther into the field, sat down again and buried her face in her hands.

I do not have to follow her, I told myself. I could get up and walk casually back through that door over there, on to my next class. This is not my problem. *She* is no longer my problem, is she? But, shaking my head, I called out to her. "Lynn, wait." I plopped down next to her again, curling up into a similar ball. "What is it?"

"Are those . . . those *things* safe?" Her voice was so choked I could barely hear her.

"What things?" My words were not fully mine. I was pursuing this, whatever it was, even though I knew, deep down, that I should not.

She looked at me then, her face wet and contorted. "Those things he uses? Are they safe? Were you ever worried . . . about getting . . . you know . . . pregnant?"

My stomach flip-flopped and the inside of my throat contracted so much, I had to gasp for breath. Answering her was impossible. Being so near to her made my fists clench and want to hit. I couldn't believe this was happening.

I stood up and took a few stiff-legged steps away from

120

where she sat. The thought of Peter intruded, and I tried to push it away with all the force I had in me. Because just then thinking about him brought the image of him with Lynn, limbs entangled, mouths and bodies pressed together. I shivered and wrapped my arms around my middle. How could he? So soon. Where? In his car, where there were surely still traces of me — a lost earring, some Kleenex, a gum wrapper.

"Don't hate me, Mandy." Lynn was standing behind me now. The whimper in her voice seemed designed to get my sympathy. Maybe that way she figured it would be Peter I'd hate most, not her. "I didn't want to have to ask you," she continued, "but I'm worried sick. Who else could I ask? My mother? She won't talk to me about periods — late or any other kind. I know I've never been all that regular, but this time . . . I just don't know."

I looked at her squarely in the face, and she winced. I had never noticed before how really pathetic she could be. Just a late period, and she had to talk to *me* about it. Me, of all people. No matter how panicked, I'd never have done this to her. And I couldn't help but wonder how long, exactly, it had taken her to give in to Peter? One date? Two? Had he gloated afterward — "See, Mandy, *she* did it."

"Mandy, can't you say something?" Lynn asked. "You must have gone through this before. You must —"

"No, as a matter of fact, I didn't. I never did. Got that? *I never did.*"

She stared at me. The air above the playing field shimmered with an unnatural heat, something we seemed

121

to be generating without much help from the October sun. "You mean . . ." She didn't bother to finish.

I turned away, seeking a cooler place on the field. She must have run back into school. I heard the bell, but I did not move again until a girls' gym class spilled noisily from the building and out onto the field. One of the girls nearly knocked me over. "Hey!" I shouted at her back. "Watch it." But she got me moving again, back into the school and to the office for a tardy slip.

The class after lunch shocked me back to the reality of school with a test that everyone seemed to know about except me. I wandered through the multiple choice questions, reading them in the most superficial way possible and choosing those answers that contained the most appealing words. This is fun, I thought. I'm flunking a test and it's giving me a high. By concentrating on the marks my pencil made on the paper I managed to obscure, for the hour, the sight of Lynn's distraught face.

The next couple of hours slipped by me in much the same way. I proceeded with my emotional blinders intact until Rachel confronted me at the end of the day, worry puckering her forehead. "You look awful, girl. Pale and blotchy. But *not* sick, that's my guess. You'd better come home with me today. We need to talk."

"Why?"

"Why?" she mimicked me in a pinched voice. "Because going home to your father in this condition won't do either one of you any good. What on earth's the matter with you, anyway?"

"I'd better call Dad to let him know where I'm going." We tried, from the office, but he wasn't in the house.

"Call him from my house," Rachel instructed and we walked, in silence, to her bus.

Tracy waved at us and we sat behind her. I stared out the window, half listening to their conversation and half replaying mine with Lynn.

"Come on, Rachel, go with me to my workshop tomorrow," Tracy said. "You might learn something."

Are those things safe? What things?

"Tracy, take notes. Honest, I'll read them and we can talk. I just can't get into those . . ."

. . . things he uses . . . ever worried about getting . . . ?

"Come on," Tracy insisted. "You've never given these people much of a chance."

. . . about getting pregnant?

"They'll get all touchy-feely, right? That's what I can't stand. You know how I hate that, Tracy. It's so phony."

Don't hate me, Mandy.

Tracy and Rachel were silent, and I realized they were staring at me. "You okay, Mandy?" Tracy asked.

"No, of course she's not," Rachel snapped. "But she doesn't need your little group grope either."

Tracy shrugged and turned around. I noticed, as if it were the most significant detail of the day, that she had trimmed at least two inches from her hair. The ends looked freshly blunt, relieved of weight and damage.

"We're here." Rachel wrapped her hands around my arm and we stood up together.

The first thing we did when we got inside her house was call Dad again.

He answered after an uncountable number of rings. I

had begun to string them like beads inside my head.

"I'm at Rachel's," I told him.

"Should I come pick you up?"

I looked vaguely at Rachel, whose ear had been pressed to the receiver, and she shook her head. "I'll take you home in a while," she whispered.

I gave her the phone so she could tell that to Dad.

"Mandy, I am your friend," Rachel said after she had hung up. "You know that, don't you?"

I nodded and for some bizarre reason wanted to laugh, but I stuffed the feeling back inside, along with everything else.

Rachel was beginning to come out from behind her funny faces and flippant remarks once again. Her dark eyes were pleading with me. What, I wondered, was it that she wanted? She wanted to talk, right? Lynn had wanted to talk too. About what? Pregnancy.

Apparently my words weren't staying neatly inside where I wanted them. The word *pregnancy* must have spilled out, because Rachel gasped and grabbed me by the shoulders tight enough to bruise. "My god, is that what's wrong with you? Mandy, you're not, are you?"

I shook my head.

"Don't, for crying out loud, scare me like that." She loosened her grip on me but did not let go entirely. "I think you're flipping out, you know that? You scared me half to death. What did you mean by saying that word, even. Never mind — wait 'til we get upstairs to my room."

She showed me the way, and I immediately lay down on her bed, where she could fuss over me in earnest and

124

in private. "Want something to drink? Some fruit? Chicken soup, maybe?"

She laughed and plopped herself alongside me. "My mom's a big nonbeliever in chicken soup, by the way. She says most of it contains some kind of acid that poisons the blood. I think she just had a bad experience with a chicken once when she was a kid — pecked or something."

She looked at me. I stared at the wall.

"Our rabbi, he's convinced my mom's trying to undermine the-family-as-we-have-known-it-for-thousands-of-years. Whenever he sees her, he gets this mournful look in his face and shakes his head."

I turned to her, my mouth tight, teeth cutting into my lips.

"My dad doesn't listen to the rabbi, or anyone else for that matter. He says he's an informed skeptic. His favorite food is pizza with everything. Want some pizza?"

My mouth opened as I exhaled. "Rachel . . ."

She leaned toward me.

"Please help me."

"Thought you'd never ask."

I sat up slowly, not letting my eyes stray from hers, reaching for the clarity, the openness, her eyes seemed to invite. "Rachel, it's like this." I took a deep breath and began to talk very rapidly. "Peter and I had a very intense physical thing, you know, but we never, well, actually went all the way. He wanted to, of course, and so did I in a way. But that last night — the night we broke up?"

Rachel nodded.

"He was really pressuring me and I was so tempted, Rachel. I came so close but then it . . . then we had this awful fight instead, about how we really felt about each other and how I was sort of waiting . . . for something. For some*thing* or some*one* else, I don't know."

Rachel covered her eyes with one hand. That stopped me cold until she uncovered them again.

"He got really ticked off, of course, and said some nasty things back and, well, that was it. Sort of."

"What do you mean?"

"Well, I can't seem to get him out of my system. He was so much a part of my life and everyone seems to think I was nuts to give him up and —"

"Forget what everyone seems to think."

"— and then Lynn . . ." I expelled so much breath that I had to wait for my lungs to fill up again before I could go on. "Lynn . . ."

"She picked up where you left off? They've been tripping the light fantastic together?"

I looked at her and burst into laughter in spite of myself. "Rachel, I swear. The way you put things sometimes."

We sat in silence for a few moments.

"The jerk," Rachel mumbled.

"Peter? Is he? I mean, is it him?"

"Of course it is. *And* Lynn." Rachel lurched off the bed and stood with her hands on her hips. "She's really something. You two were pretty good friends, weren't you? How could you stand such an idiot?"

"I can't really blame her for assuming that Peter and

I had been — Well, she's so crazy about him, she'd do anything he asked anyway."

"Exactly."

"But he's older and he's male and I've been, I suppose, pretty frustrating for him, sexually and all that."

"Okay, so now we can pin the blame on Peter's glands. At least that's better than *your* feeling somehow responsible."

"Well, really, Rachel. It's natural, with Lynn so eager to please. . . ."

"Natural maybe. That doesn't make it right. How can you keep defending them like this?" She paused and then, quietly, asked, "And she's pregnant now?"

"No. I doubt it. She's just worried about getting pregnant. My gosh, how could she even have had *time?* And why talk to me about it?"

Rachel threw her hands into the air and began to pace in and out of a sunlit square on her rug. Her whole color and manner seemed to change from inside the square to outside it. I watched her shift from glistening yellow to dusky gray, back and forth.

"Rachel, I —"

"Sh-sh-sh. I'm trying to think." Her fingers raked energetically through her hair, a gesture I now recognized as more than a nervous one. It seemed to help her think, as if her fingertips could stick to and draw out the best her mind had to offer. "Where does old Gary fit into all this?"

"I'm not sure. I like him and I want to like him more, but it seems as if I've met him at the wrong time or something. I'm not clear of Peter yet, and Gary is so different, so hard to adjust to. But I want to keep trying."

Rachel threw her hands into the air. "Thank you, God," she said to the ceiling, "for sparing me this diabolical thing we so quaintly call love. I've suspected it all along — it's nothing but a trap."

"Trap?"

"Well, what do you call it when you're so stuck on this jerk, you can't open your eyes and see a really good guy standing right in front of you, and just have some fun! Why does everything have to be so dreadfully serious? Love triangles, pregnancy, jealousy — it's all got the ring of a soap opera if you ask me."

I looked down, studying my fingers, trying not to look hurt. I became aware, for the first time, that I needed more than her caring. I needed her respect.

"You were asking me, weren't you?" Rachel asked. "For what I'd do?"

I nodded.

"Well, okay, then. It's simple, isn't it? Leave Peter and Lynn to their business — it has nothing to do with you now, does it? You didn't want him anyway, really. Admit it. And then you can go on to better things."

"Like Gary?"

"No, like yourself."

"Yes, well, I can see you doing that. But I'm not like you. I wish I were, but I'm not."

"Yes, you are. What do you mean?"

"You're so . . . so independent."

"Listen, you want to see dependence? You should

128

stick around and see me with my dad. All he has to do is hint at a criticism of me and I'm oatmeal. It's the most disgusting kind of dependence."

"I don't believe you."

Rachel tried to laugh off this topic but she was, to my surprise, fighting back tears.

"Well, I'll believe you if you want me to. About your dad, but —"

"Mandy, just last night at supper. It was so typical. My dad watched me eat. He always watches me eat. And he just can't seem to resist saying something. Last night it was 'Slow down. If you do, then you won't eat so much.'

"So naturally I could hardly swallow what was in my mouth at the time. I nearly choked trying to get this darn piece of meat down. Then he sort of smirks, looks over at my mom and says, 'Shouldn't she be rid of that baby fat by now?'"

"What did she say?"

Rachel was blinking, her eyes drying rapidly and regaining their sharpness. "My mother? What does that matter? She probably pinched my cheek and said my baby fat is cute. The point is, I hang on every word that man says. I can't help believing him and wanting him to . . . to . . . oh, I don't know. Approve, I guess. We have these kinds of scenes every day. If it's not my weight, it's my hair, or my grades, or my social life."

I wished I could approach her father and tell him to lay off. Tell him his daughter is so perfect, why can't he see it?

"Now do you believe me? Especially if I tell you that I adore him, no matter how often he makes me cry. Real schizo, huh?"

"I believe you, but that doesn't make me stop wanting to be like you. Your father's the problem, not you."

A long pause followed. On the turned-down radio, Paul McCartney started crooning "Yesterday." Together, spontaneously, we sang "All my troubles seemed so far away." I smiled and Rachel let go with a roaring, relieved laugh.

"Rachel," I said. "I really like you. You know that?"

She nodded. "I like you too. Feeling better?"

"Sure, I guess so." It was easy to laugh along with her, but I wished, deep down, that I could stay there in her room, safe for the rest of my life.

"Come on. I'll get you home. Your dad sounded worried. Kind of . . . oh, I don't know. Needy, I guess. Maybe if you concentrate on him for a while . . ."

"That's what Mom said."

Rachel glanced at me, trying not to look alarmed.

"I mean, what she always used to say."

The drive home seemed to go too fast. Rachel chattered away about our Homecoming plans. I was surprised to learn that this would be her first. "First and last," she said. "I've been trying to figure out what's in it for Mark."

I shook my head and smiled. "He likes you, Rachel. If you weren't so afraid of 'traps' and stuff, you'd be able to see that and enjoy it."

"Never mind, girl. You've convinced me today. Nothing serious 'til I'm thirty, at least."

I spotted it before we'd even turned into the driveway — the light blue peeked through our huge ever-
greens, and I thought my eyes were playing their usual
tricks on me. But Rachel slowed down after turning into
our driveway; she'd seen Peter's car too. "Is that who I
think it is?"

I nodded.

"Want me to turn around, or what?"

Without realizing it, I had slid down into my seat,
my chin against my collarbone, my knees bent and raised.
I was hiding. I felt as if I were five-years-old again and
slouched under the window, hiding from the mailman
because I'd put a piece of raw chicken in the mailbox to
see if the summer sun would bake it like my mom's
oven did. It had sat in there rotting until the mailman
complained to my parents about me. It wasn't the first
surprise I had left in the mailbox for him, he had claimed,
but he'd gotten me mixed up with some other kid on his
route.

"Mandy? What do you want me to do?" Rachel asked.

"Huh?" I sat up.

"Where should I go?"

"There, I guess. Right next to his car."

She did as I asked, leaving the engine idling and still
seeming to wait for instructions from me.

Then the porch door swung open and Peter emerged,
followed by my dad. Peter stopped when he saw
Rachel's car; he couldn't have recognized it. Then he
spotted me. His grin was automatic and sincere-look-
ing, but then, as if thinking twice about it, he took it
back.

He needed a haircut, I noticed. Otherwise, he looked good. Not pale and haggard. Not languishing without me. No, of course not. Why should he? In fact, I told myself, he's never looked better. His stance had always tended to tilt to one side, as though his angular body were preparing to propel itself in the opposite direction from what was expected. Now I saw him definitely leaning away from me.

I sat up straighter and opened my car door. "Thanks, Rachel."

In confusion, she turned off the car, then started it again. "Sure. See you tomorrow."

Slamming the door, I approached the porch steps, anger and, for some reason, embarrassment heating up my face to the tips of my ears. Dad looked behind him and to each side as if in search for whatever was wrong with everybody. His forced smile didn't survive. Peter and I scarcely took our eyes off each other. I imagined that my eyes were telling him what was all too clear to me now — "We are finished after all. That's that."

Peter opened his mouth as if to speak and then averted his eyes and jammed his hands into his jeans pockets. Finally I maneuvered around him and into the house. The whole thing couldn't have taken more than a few seconds, but I felt it in slow motion.

Rachel's car pulled away from the house then, a few seconds later, Peter's. I wished I could have said even half of what I had wanted to say to him. But I was emotionally out of control and I worried that Dad might get some ricochets. He should not, after all, be involved in this. I was living my own life. But why, I wondered, did this freedom of mine, which was supposed to taste so sweet, feel like a throat full of tacks?

12 ⤇

THE KNOCK on my door a few minutes later was so light it could have been the wood expanding or contracting on its own. I had a hard time imagining the sound coming from my dad's oversized knuckles. "I'm asleep," I said.

"Mandy, can I come in? Are you . . . ?"

He wants to say *decent*, I thought, but was too embarrassed. When had he become so awkward, so tentative? "Come on in, Dad."

The door opened and he stood half in and half out of my room. "You want something?"

For a moment I wondered if he thought I had called for him. "Nothing, really. Thanks."

"It *is* suppertime," he said. "We should eat something."

I was relieved that the subject was food. "Are you hungry?"

"Not especially. Are you? There are some store-bought cookies down there. And some bread and some cheese crackers and . . ." His voice trailed away like an increasingly illegible grocery list.

Cookies, I thought. Cheese crackers. I laughed. "Mom would d ——"

He looked at me in alarm.

"She'd have a fit," I corrected. "Food was so important to her."

He nodded, the alarm not quite fading. In fact, his face was quickly closing to me like a curtain — one of those curtains that used to pull back from movie theatre screens. Not the first, heavy one, but the second, filmy one whose pleats bent and darkened whatever was on the screen below it.

"I suppose BLTs would be okay again," he commented, as if to himself.

"How about just LTs?"

"What?"

"We finished the bacon last night, Dad."

"We did?"

All our conversations lately seemed to have more questions than answers. "Maybe we can toss together a salad," I said. "I know we've got everything we need for that."

He nodded and started to leave my room. "I'll be back in a half hour or so. Just want to walk around, before the sun goes."

"Want some company?" This question slipped out and I immediately regretted it. Why couldn't we just leave each other alone? Soon I would be out of his hair, at college, and maybe then we could simply proceed by remembering our own better times.

We left the house and headed for the nearest field. Our driveway went downhill from the house and turned into a dirt road that stretched all the way to the outer edge of our farm, to the large hill that used to be pastures and now bore the burden of expensive houses. The dirt road divided our fields neatly in two, and we followed it until its first dip, down to a vast tomato patch.

"How was the card club, by the way? I kept meaning to ask all week, but . . ."

"Not bad. Not bad at all. It brought back . . . well, memories. But they were such good ones. It was okay."

"Are you going again next month?"

He nodded. "It's time, I guess."

Dad crouched to examine some late blight on his tomatoes. "Do you want to tell me what's going on between you and Peter?" he asked at last.

"What did your buddy, Peter, tell you?" I felt my face flush with anger all over again.

Dad scowled at me, more irritated than I had seen him in weeks.

"I'm sure he told you all about things. Why should you want to hear my side?" I hoped that Dad would somehow realize that it was Peter I was angry with, not him.

Dad scooped a handful of dry, gray dirt and rubbed it through his hands pensively. Then he examined his palms; the dirt had lodged in some crevices. He looked up at me, a calmer expression in his blue eyes.

Mom had told me once that she had long suspected Dad's eyes of having hypnotic powers. Why else, she had asked, would he have been able to win her love so quickly, so effortlessly? She had started teaching school,

136

what she had always wanted to do, and suddenly she was a farmer's wife instead, sweating and lugging and worrying over weather right alongside her husband.

I knew Dad tended to blame himself for Mom's early death, as if she were some fragile plant he had been unable to shield from nature's batterings. But Mom had not been in the least bit fragile and only something with the power of cancer could have defeated her.

"Never mind all that," Dad said, standing up and brushing off his hands on his trousers.

I wasn't sure what he was telling me to "never mind." Had he been thinking about Mom too?

But he added, "Your love life is none of my business."

"Well, whatever Peter —"

"Peter didn't tell me a thing. In fact," Dad said a bit gruffly, "you weren't mentioned once."

"Oh." I tried to shrug. "I think it's over, Dad. That's all. You know Homecoming's tomorrow?"

Dad shook his head.

I cleared my throat. "Well, it is. And he's . . . Peter's taking someone else."

Dad did not look as surprised as I had expected.

"It's Lynn," I added. "I think they've been having this . . . thing about each other for quite some time."

Dad looked so accepting of my half-true explanations that I continued. "Rachel lined me up with a guy for the dance. We're doubling."

We started to walk again. I followed his lead back toward the house. "Blind date, then?" he asked.

Here's my chance, I thought. I can claim I've never met Gary. Then if Dad hits the roof, it will be Rachel's fault, not mine. But I reminded myself that independent people did not need to blame things on good friends, or lie, or even explain themselves at all if they didn't want to.

"Not exactly," I said. "I met him a couple of times. Nice guy. His name's Gary." I wanted to tell him Gary was black. I really did, but I couldn't think of the right words. The kind of words Mom might use.

"Well, I'm glad you're going," he said. "I know how much those dances mean to you girls. Your brothers never seemed to care much, or I guess Sam did, didn't he?" He shook his head as if to jog memories into their proper slots.

"I'm sorry, Dad."

"About what?"

"Peter and . . . everything, I guess." Tears sprang into my eyes without any warning. I was sure Dad would not see them, but I kept my face down all the same. "You'd probably just as soon see me end up with him, wouldn't you? It would feel kind of safe and . . . natural?"

He shook his head. "No, not really." Grinning at me, he added, "Didn't you know that, to a father, nobody's good enough for his little girl?"

"No, I guess I didn't." I bristled, at first, at the "little girl" remark. But then, with a deep breath, I plunged in further. "You've always liked Peter so much, though."

"Yes, that's true. But . . . well, he's too old for you,

138

for one thing. Too ready to settle down. And, for another, he'll never be much of a provider, I suspect."

I nodded in ready agreement, hoping he wasn't just
trying to make me, and himself, feel better.

"Who knows?" he said brightly. "Maybe this Gary
will be the one for you."

I could see that he was trying so hard to console me
and be more like his old self that it was beginning to
exhaust us both. I swallowed. "Uh . . . Dad?" But again,
the words eluded me. Mom, I begged, help me with
this. "Dad, I have this friend who's . . . been going out
with a . . . a black guy. A really neat guy, but they're
not serious or anything. What do you think about that?"

Dad had listened to me carefully, his eyes on me more
than on the road as we walked. "Well, now . . ."

"I guess what I'm asking is for your opinion as a father, but also as a broad-minded person, you know?"

He shook his head. "Mandy, I think you know how
I'd feel if I were her father. It doesn't . . . sit right with
me. I have nothing against black people, but mixed
marriages are such a messy —"

"There's no question about marriage, Dad."

"There's *always* that question. Believe me. Marriage
is hard enough without extra problems like that. People,
other people, can be real hateful about this sort of thing.
And then there're the children involved . . ."

"Dad, for heaven's sake. Who said anything about
children? This is 1969, not the dark ages. The civil rights
movement has made such a dif——"

"If you're her friend, I'd say you should advise her

139

not to date him anymore. I know if I were her
father —"

"Okay, Dad. I'll talk to her."

"— I'd forbid it. Plain and simple."

Too far. I'd carried it too far. The word *forbid* left no
question, no area for negotiation.

We were back to our porch steps already. Dad sat
down on the top step and looked around. "Nice night.
Too nice to go inside."

I sat next to him and followed his gaze.

"As long as we're talking about . . . tough things, in
general terms, that is, I wonder if you've ever thought
about what's going to happen to this place? When I'm
gone, I mean."

There was something in his question that chilled me.
"No," I answered, although I had often wondered. "Sam
and Greg sure don't want it, do they?"

Dad shook his head. "No, they're scattered now. Even
starting families, which is as it should be. We can barely
get them to come home for holidays, it seems like. They
don't miss this place."

"They miss us, Dad. I know they do." But I agreed
with him about the farm. It was part of what they had
put behind them, in a tidy package, to be opened, perhaps, when they were old and had grandchildren bal-
anced in their laps. I could picture Greg, especially,
recounting, "When I was your age . . ." And then would
come the images of backbreaking work, of heroics, of
bumper crops followed closely by lost ones, Technicolor
pictures of the farm, *their* farm all of a sudden. I wondered if I would do the same.

"Want to hear something funny?" Dad asked. "I always hoped you might marry a farmer and stay on here."

"Me?"

"Sure. It sounds crazy, of course, now, but . . . that was one thing about Peter. He always seemed to like this place. He had a special feel for it." Dad cleared his throat and clenched his hands together. "Now I'm not sure what we . . . what I should do."

I groaned. What exactly did he want from me? I longed to be close to him again, but how could I on his terms? He really wanted to keep me here. His little girl. He would hand me over to a husband but then oversee our lives right along with those of his crops.

As much as I'd always loved the farm, I was terrified by his fantasy. It gave me the same gut-tightening and cold sweat reaction that I'd had to Peter's habit of neatly plotting the course of our lives together. As if I should share his dreams before I could gather together some of my own.

If Dad had meant to soothe my feelings about Peter, all he'd really managed to do was strengthen my resolve to be on my own. I was going out with whomever I pleased, regardless of what color he was or even, for that matter, what character he possessed. It was *my* life, not Dad's, and not Peter's.

"Dad, I don't want . . . that is, you really have to let me . . ."

"I know, I know. I have to let you go. Not depend on you so much. It's only fair. Maybe you're not ready to talk about the future of this place yet. I guess I'll be around awhile yet, huh? I'm not exactly an old fogey."

"Dad, about this guy . . . my date."

"Hey, that's okay, Mandy. I know I'm not much good at talking over this kind of thing. I suppose you'll talk it over with . . . you know, your mother."

I followed his gaze, which seemed to focus on the silo, or maybe he was trying to look straight through the stone walls. "I thought you disapproved of that. My talking to her."

"We do what we have to do."

I sighed and tucked my fingers into the crook of his arm. He was right about that, at least — we do what we have to do. And the easiest thing to do, for the moment, was to play his little girl. Nothing wrong with old games if they make someone else feel good for a while.

"Want me to make you an omelet?" I asked, hoping he would remember how our game went.

"A Spanish omelet?" he asked on cue.

"You bet."

"Green pepper?"

"Check."

"Tomato?"

"Check."

"Four eggs?"

"Check check check check." We hadn't played this for years, not since I was the age when monotony is so reassuring.

"No, thanks," he shifted gears. "Got any vegetable soup?"

"You bet."

"Carrots?"

"Check. . . ."

The sun sank at last. It looked tired of sustaining such a complicated and colorful warmth. Just as we were both tired of sustaining ours. But October would be giving way soon to the simpler purity of November and December. Things would fall into place for a long rest, and I would be making my own decisions accordingly.

*

When the phone rang an hour or so later, I let Dad answer. He spoke for a few moments and then came to me. "It's Peter. He wants to talk to you."

I stared at the TV. Dad and I had been watching a movie, and I pretended to be totally engrossed in it. But a commercial intruded.

"Mandy. Answer the phone. Now." Dad's voice was too weary for me to argue with it.

I dragged my wobbly legs to the phone. "Hello?"

"Hi. Uh, how ya doing?"

"Fine."

"Good." Peter took an audibly deep breath. "Listen, is it too late for me to come over?"

"You mean tonight?"

"Yeah."

"Well . . . I'm watching this movie with Dad. It's —"

"Mandy, can I come over? Please?" His protective layer of jauntiness was being rapidly stripped away. I wondered if he had been drinking or something. He sounded so strange. "Can I?" he asked again.

I waited for my answer along with him. "No, I don't think so. Not tonight."

He seemed to be giving me a chance to change my

mind. There was such a prolonged silence, it occurred to me that we might have been disconnected. Maybe he had passed out. I tried to hear signs of life through my receiver — the inhale and exhale of a cigarette, the drumming of his fingertips, background music, probably his favorite recording of the bluesy trumpet solo "I Can't Get Started" — but I could hear nothing. Just as I was about to hang up, I heard him take another deep breath.

"I want . . ." he said, his voice soft as a brush of the skin, "I want you."

I closed my eyes and leaned against the wall, which began to undulate sickeningly. I swallowed a few times. I tried but could not seem to grasp the contours of his face in my mind, the colors of him. All I could grasp at the moment was a picture of Lynn's face, distorted by her fear, confusion, anger, humiliation. She could be in her room right now, I thought, perhaps staring at herself in the mirror. Examining her belly. Trying to see through flesh. Trying to understand what had happened, and why. Waiting for her period to come (which I was fairly sure it would) so it could solve everything. Except that it would solve only one problem. The rest would still be out there, out of immediate reach, for her to rearrange. For *us*, to rearrange.

Without another sound, I gently settled the receiver back into its cradle. I waited for the phone to ring again, but only for a minute. I doubted he would call again. If he did, I was afraid I might have to answer, with some small twinge of a voice from somewhere I hadn't explored yet, "I want you too."

144

13 ⌇

LYNN WAS IN SCHOOL the next day, looking more cheerful, and I wanted to ask her if she had gotten her period, but it seemed inappropriate. Besides, she didn't give me a chance.

"Hi," Rachel said from behind me.

I was staring at Lynn, way ahead of me in the lunch line. "Hi, Rachel. Can you eat with me today?"

"Sure, if I butt in line. Sorry," she said to some kids behind me. "But fat people have a much more urgent need for nourishment."

"Stop all that fat talk," I said absently, still watching Lynn. She was actually laughing, thank goodness. Shelley Bingham was with her and gave me a funny look, so I turned to Rachel. "You're not fat, you know."

"I know. I just need to hear other, skinnier people say that every now and then for reassurance. 'Rachel, you are gorgeous' is another favorite of mine. It takes so little to elicit compliments from people. Ever notice that?"

I sighed. "Notice what?"

"You sure are far-off today. Are you going to tell me what happened yesterday after I left or do I have to use my lurid imagination?"

"Well, there's not much to tell. I'm sorry if I'm a little out of it today. I'm just thinking things over. Trying to make some reasonable decisions and then stick with them."

Rachel nodded.

"Also, he called last night."

"Who, Gary? Peter? Prince Charles? Can't keep track anymore."

"Peter. He wanted to see me, but I said no."

Rachel widened her eyes at me. "No? Just like that?"

"I wanted to try to tell him why, but I just couldn't. It's all too complicated. Lynn and Gary and all."

"Hey, but you resisted the easy thing, which would have been to say, 'Come on over and let's forget all this fuss.' "

"Yeah, I guess so. I did do the right thing, didn't I? I'm leaving the two of them alone, like you said. It's not my business anymore."

"Thatta girl. Great. So let's just concentrate on tonight."

"Tonight?"

"The dance. Remember? Are you kidding?"

"Oh, that."

Rachel flipped a nonchalant hand at me. "Oh, that. Just another social event of the season. Ho hum."

I giggled. "Can you help me look good again?" For an instant I wished she could completely disguise me, but I didn't know why.

"Sure, but we'd better do it at your house, and then Mark and Gary can pick us up there."

"I suppose that's best. Dad knows I'm going. He'll want to meet Gary."

"Of course he will." She eyed me suspiciously. "You did tell him about Gary, didn't you?"

"Well, sort of," I said. I hated lying to Rachel, but I didn't want her to know what a coward I was.

I took a lunch tray and filled it, muttering the usual complaints about the food.

Rachel did not ask about Dad again. Instead, she asked, "Did you get a new dress?"

"No, did you?" I was amazed that I hadn't thought about that earlier. So much for thinking things through.

We found two places at a table, isolated ourselves from the rowdies farther down and ate without enthusiasm.

"I'll tell you what," Rachel said. "I've got this great dress for you. Actually, I've never worn it myself. It's a size seven and I thought it would inspire me to eternal skinniness."

I discreetly eyed her figure across from me. She was probably an eleven, sometimes a nine.

"I know, I know. It was pure insanity on my part. I'd practically put the dumb thing out of my mind, but there you sit, a perfect size seven, and too dippy to have thought about what you're going to wear tonight. I'll bring it when I come over."

"Are you sure it will fit? What color is it and stuff?"

"Trust me. It will fit. You're about my height — five feet five, right? Good. The length will be fine. It's a royal blue knit. It'll be smashing."

"Thanks, Rachel."

"No sweat."

*

The royal blue made my eyes look more definite, like Dad's, only darker. Rachel did her magic with my hair and face, and then we started on hers. I marveled again at the natural clean lines of her face, the perfect features. Her eyebrows reminded me of Ali MacGraw's.

"I wish I had your eyebrows," I said as she was straightening them out with a tiny, caterpillary brush. "They give you a very forceful look."

"You mean," Rachel said as she lightly lined her eyelids, upper and lower, "if a weirdo confronts me, all I have to do is brandish my eyebrows and he'll leave me alone?"

"Absolutely. Maybe I could borrow your eyebrows tonight if Gary and I get some nasty looks. But I don't think kids our age have any problem with — Rachel?"

"Hm-m-m?"

"What do you think of Gary and me. As a couple, I mean? Do you see anything wrong with it?"

She shook her head. "Not me. You're worried about your dad, aren't you? 'Cause you didn't tell him?"

"Wouldn't you be?"

"I worry about my dad no matter what I'm doing. I'm the wrong person to ask about that."

"Well, I think it will be okay. I've really grown up a lot lately and he must realize that. I'm responsible for what I do, not him."

"Thatta girl. What can he say, in front of Mark and

me and God and everybody? Besides, he seems like a pretty sharp, with-it kind of guy to me."

"Sharp, yes. I'm not so sure about 'with-it.' But he'll have to be, won't he?"

"Phone for Rachel," Dad called from downstairs.

We both jumped; neither of us had even heard it ring.

"Probably my dad," Rachel said as she left my room. "To see if I remembered my deodorant."

A few seconds later, Dad's knock on my open door startled me again. "You are . . . you look really . . . very nice. New dress?"

"It's Rachel's. Isn't she something?"

"I've got to admit she's an improvement over Lynn."

See, I wanted to say to him, how good my choices have been lately? Keep that in mind for a while. . . .

Dad examined the edge of my door, rubbing it with his fingers as if he were slowly, carefully, sanding the surface.

"Dad?"

"Yes?"

"Gary — my date, is well, different." I wanted to kick myself for being such a coward.

"Private-school type, huh?"

"Excuse me, please, Mr. Smetana." Rachel bounced back into the room.

"Well, I'll let you girls finish getting ready. Sure you don't want to eat? A sandwich doesn't seem enough. . . ."

"We're sure, Dad. See you downstairs in a few minutes."

I asked Rachel who had called.

"Just Mark. Forgot what time we'd finally settled on."

"Oh. Dad liked the dress. I told him it was yours."

"Of course. Impeccable taste. He's all right, your dad."

We finished getting ready and were feeling in a pretty festive mood by the time the doorbell rang. "I'd better answer that," I said, rushing ahead of Rachel down the stairs.

"Hi," I said to the two dressed-up guys at the door. In the dim light, it appeared they wore almost identical dark suits. But Gary's shirt was pale blue whereas Mark's was white. Gary looked impressive and comfortable at the same time, and I wondered how he managed that.

I felt Dad behind me and I looked back at him just as his confused gaze was moving back and forth between Mark and Gary. Then he extended his hand tentatively toward Mark. "Hello, Gary?"

"No, sir. I'm Mark Springer."

"Dad, this is Gary Jefferson. Gary, my dad."

They shook hands and my dad looked amiable enough until I spotted the rigidity of his jaw, the strain of tension in his neck. Rachel was somewhere behind us. Gary gave me an odd look and then proceeded to discuss the house and farm with Dad. Mark seemed extremely amused by the whole scene.

I squeezed myself out of the middle of things and went to find my purse and coat.

"Mandy?" Dad was somehow behind me again, whispering so nobody else could hear.

I turned around.

He stared at me a moment, looking more disappointed than angry.

"Dad, I —"

"We'll talk later" was all he said, and then he was back by the door, politely saying his good-byes and have-a-good-times.

"Phew," Mark said once we were secure in his car. He started the engine and headed for the school.

Gary was quiet beside me. In the front seat, Rachel started chattering nervously with Mark. When we were almost there, when the two in front were engaged in a lively conversation, Gary turned to me and whispered, "Why didn't you tell him?"

"What?"

"You know what I mean. I've seen that look often enough. He wanted Mark to be your date so bad it was pathetic."

"I'm sorry." I paused, for a few seconds actually considering a mere apology enough. "It's just that I was afraid if I told him ahead of time, he wouldn't let me go. He's not racist, honest. It's just . . . well, I figured once he met you, he wouldn't mind. I'll talk to him tomorrow. It'll be all right. He's a great guy. You two will . . ." I ran out of steam.

Gary did not look satisfied.

For the first time since I'd met him and decided to invite him to Homecoming, I wondered exactly what I was doing and why. I hated that renewed sense of bewilderment. Things had seemed so clear the day before.

"Gary, I don't know if you can understand this, but

honestly, it seems like nothing I've done since . . . since I lost my mom makes much sense for very long. I know that's a lousy excuse for putting you on the spot like that, but my dad and I aren't communicating very well lately and I just didn't . . . get around to telling him about you." Is that true, I wondered?

He took my hand into his and stroked it gently. "That's okay. I guess I can understand lousy communication all right. My mom and I haven't really talked in months."

"Here we are," Mark said over his shoulder to us. I realized that he and Rachel had been listening to us.

"I'm forgiven, then?" I whispered to Gary.

"Forgiven." Gary let go of my hand, and we headed for the school.

14 ✎

THE DANCE WAS WELL under way when we arrived. The school gym looked somehow weary and embarrassed by the predictable burden of crepe paper, balloons and damp bodies. "Not again," it seemed to murmur.

Gary touched my elbow as we headed toward the refreshment table. I searched frantically for Peter and Lynn, hoping to find them first so I could more effectively avoid them. Gary handed me a glass of punch and asked if I'd been to many of these dances.

"No. Well, yes, I suppose. They're fun after a while, it always seems to me. But at first, deadly."

Gary smiled and nodded. "I know what you mean. Nobody really knows the proper thing to be doing, so some of us do nothing at all and others act up. I remember my first one, back in junior high. I sweated through my suit so bad, Mom nearly had to toss it."

"You did?"

"Why do you look so surprised?"

"I don't know. You just seem like the kind of person who always knows exactly what to do."

"I'm pretty good at faking it. Wait 'til you dance with me — you'll have to touch my clammy hands."

Rachel joined us. "Mark's over there talking with some bore he used to know. Couldn't stand another minute of catching up on what so-and-so's doing now and where what's-his-name is going to school next year. What were you two talking about? Don't let me interrupt."

"We were talking about . . . sweat, actually," I said.

"What?"

We all laughed. Just then I spotted Peter. He saw me at about the same time. Lynn was at his side looking very happy. Peter turned toward her to say something, but his eyes remained on me. Then I caught him searching, apparently for my date. Rachel and Gary were talking next to me.

I nodded when Gary said something that sounded like it deserved a nod, still conscious of Peter's eyes and still unsure what to do.

Just then, the band started up and Gary put his arm around me to guide me toward the dance floor.

Peter's arm encircled Lynn's waist and then all I could see was his back. He was wearing his navy blue blazer. I must have seen him in it a hundred times before.

Gary and I were dancing a slow dance. He smelled of wool, starch and shave cream. No cologne or after-shave. I liked that, no pretense. I tried to concentrate exclusively on the terrific person I happened to be with, and yet my eyes kept searching out a familiar blue blazer.

After an hour or so, I had persuaded myself to ignore Peter and Lynn, and I really began to enjoy myself. "See

154

that teacher over there," I said. "The blond woman, uptight-looking?"

Gary nodded and then rested his cheek against the side of my head. The band was big on slow dances, and I was glad.

"Her name's Miss Winston. Speech teacher. And she starts out every one of her new classes with a lecture on how obnoxious it is to cut your fingernails with a clipper. I swear. She actually asks for a show of hands, for who is tacky enough to use such a thing.

" 'That horrible sound they make,' she says. 'And then those nasty little leavings. Fingernail leavings.' She shudders! It's wild. Kids take her class just to hide clippers in their pockets. Every now and then they clip off a good long thumbnail and wait to see her shudder again."

Gary laughed all the while I was telling him about Miss Winston. I felt his breath in my hair, and a couple of times he shook his head in disbelief, moving mine along with it.

When he started a story of his own about a math teacher, I was grateful, because I had just caught sight again of Peter nearby. Alone this time.

The dance ended and Gary excused himself to go to the rest room. I considered going, too, but I figured Lynn might be in there. Looking around for someone to talk with, I was startled by Peter's voice. "Hello," he said.

I smiled at him; it really did feel good to see him and that surprised me. I must be getting over him, I thought.

"Can I talk to you, please?" Peter clasped my arm just

above the elbow and guided me away from the well-lit area by the rest rooms and phone booths, toward the dim hall by the band room.

"Where's . . . Lynn?" I finally managed to say when we had stopped. "Rest room?"

He nodded. The shadowy light reminded me of that night several weeks earlier, in our front yard. The yard-light cast uneven light around us and made velvety, seductive shadows.

Peter was staring at me and I couldn't read his face at all. For a crazy instant I thought he might be about to kiss me, but then I realized that I was reverting to old times again.

"What are you staring at?" I asked, leaning against the wall.

He didn't answer. I felt pinned to the wall even though he was not touching me or giving any indication that he intended to.

"What exactly do you want?" I asked coolly. My pleasure at seeing him, hearing his sudden "hello" was slipping away fast.

He bit his lower lip. "I'm trying very hard not to get angry. I know I have no right. . . . I just want to talk, that's all."

"So talk. Let's talk. What's the topic?"

"How about that guy you're with? He's not from this school, is he?"

"He goes to the Academy. As if my date were any of your business anyway. Maybe you expected me to sit at home."

156

He bit his lip again. "I don't know what I expected. No, of course, I wouldn't want you to —"

"You're bothered by him, aren't you? Because he's black, maybe?"

"Mandy, you know me —"

A couple wandered by us hand in hand. They did not look at us, but Peter lowered his voice. "You know me better than that."

"Well, you sure can't be jealous. You're here with my former best friend. It must be something else about my date that's bugging you."

"Come off it. How do you know if I'm jealous or —"

"Actually, Peter, I had no idea you were such a racist pig." I knew this was unfair, but I couldn't seem to stop myself. "After all the bands you've played in and all the black musicians you idolize, you really surprise and shock —"

"Stop that. He's not what's bugging me. Not exactly."

"Then, what is the problem?"

Another couple, carrying tension with them like a pet on a leash, hurried by us to find a secluded spot of their own. Hearing the shrill voice of the girl burst through, I tried to tone my own voice down. "What's the problem," I repeated.

"Well, it's — How about your dad? What did he say about this guy?"

"Nothing much."

"Hasn't he had enough to contend with lately, without you pulling this on him? This is a tough thing for people his age."

"My decision to go out with Gary had nothing to do with Dad. Or *you*."

"Oh, this isn't some rebellious little stunt of yours, huh? You're not using this guy to —"

"Using? How can you, of all people, accuse me of using people. What do you call your little fling with Lynn, if not using her?"

He moved slightly closer to me. "How? I'm not into making you jealous, if that's what you think. She's a nice girl, a friend. So what?"

I stared at him in disbelief, the anger I had felt that day with Lynn on the playing field returning in a flood. "You . . . she . . ." In frustration, I shoved him away from me with both hands. Tears rolled down my cheeks. "How *could* you? How could you go to bed with her?" I started to walk away from him, but he grabbed my arm again.

"What makes you think that?"

"Are you denying it?" I wanted to blurt out everything Lynn had said to me, emphasizing how pathetic she had appeared and how insensitive. But something stopped me — an old loyalty perhaps.

Peter still held on to my arm, his fingers moist now and, I imagined, leaving red horizontal stripes on my skin. He could not seem to think of what to say next.

"Please let go of my arm. You're hurting me. If that's what you wanted to do, okay. You succeeded."

He let go but his hand hovered nearby as if to reclaim me at any moment. "Mandy . . . I . . . I can imagine what you must be thinking but . . . I swear, I'm not using her. I wouldn't —"

158

"Oh, of course you're not," I said with an exaggerated shrug. "You're madly in love. Swept off your feet, I suppose. You've known her as long as you've known me, but suddenly, within the last couple of months, there's this passionate attraction. Enough to forget all about me and —"

"Oh, if only I could!"

"Well, do then. I don't care."

"I know you don't," he said. "Lynn *does*." He straightened up and shifted his eyes away from me. "She makes me feel like I'm something special. Can you imagine that? Me, special? Like I matter to her, more than anything or anybody else. Is it wrong of me to want that?" He turned away from me, apparently wanting to leave but not wanting to end this conversation yet. His jaws started working as though he were talking to himself.

We stayed that way for a while. I watched his back, the hair curling around his collar, the bend of his elbows. Since the lighting was poor, I was half seeing, half remembering. Every line and texture of him. I ached to be able to run my fingers across him, the way a blind person would. I remembered our first date and our first kiss, his first touch, as vividly as I recalled anything in my life. How could it be that he didn't know that?

"Peter," I said at last, wishing the tears would stop, "didn't I ever . . . make you feel that you mattered? Didn't I?"

He flipped back the sides of his jacket and jammed his hands deep into his pants pockets. In a spot of stray light from down the hall, I saw the sharp pebbly bumps of his knuckles inside the fabric.

"Because if I didn't . . . I'm sorry. I really am. I meant to. I . . ." Detaching myself from the wall and from him, I steered myself in the direction of the gym. My movements were purposeful — I wiped away at my face, trying to repair the damage to my makeup — but also dreamlike, as though I were sleepwalking.

Mom? As I mentally called her, I became suddenly aware of how silent she had been the last few days. Right when I'd needed her most. Can't you get me out of this? I begged her.

The sounds of other kids having fun at the dance were all I heard in reply.

15

"WHERE'VE YOU BEEN?" Gary looked at me, smiling at first, then scowling. "You all right? You don't look so hot."

"I was feeling a little sick," I said over the blare of the band. Bodies were gyrating around us and it seemed he was the only thing that was solid and stationary. I let his solidity become mine. "I'm sorry to have disappeared like that."

"That's okay. Feel up to dancing?"

"Sure." I was willing to do anything to forget about my conversation with Peter.

Rachel and Mark danced their way over to us. "Hey, Mandy," she said. "Thought you'd skipped out or something. Cinderella-style."

"No." A clever comeback eluded me.

Mark was staring at me, but he didn't say a word. I wondered if he'd seen me leave the gym with Peter. Or maybe Rachel had been telling him about me. I shot a defensive glance her way, but she was the picture of innocence. Then, I realized — what would she tell Mark? What exactly had I done?

I looked up at Gary's pleasant face, glazed with sweat now. "You're quiet all of a sudden," he said after the dance had ended. "Want to sit the next one out? Are you thirsty or anything?"

His solicitude made me feel all the more guilty. All the more anxious to please. "I'm fine, really. I just hope the next one's a slow dance."

He wrapped an arm around me, encouraged by my remark. I leaned against his warm body, and when the music started, it was a slow dance, seemingly just for us.

I concentrated on the steady beat, on my feet shuffling between his. His body pressed tighter against mine and it was different, better even, than that night when we had danced to "The Sounds of Silence." I recognized the tingling of quiet excitement and smiled to myself.

Hold on, I thought. Careful. I forced myself to focus on the words of the song. Every syllable of every word. Safely curling up with someone else's romantic lament, the finding of love, the loss of it and finding it again. Almost always the same. Sentimental junk, really, I told myself. But I wanted it to be true. I wanted to try again, and maybe do it better. Maybe I *could* make someone feel special and still not surrender completely to him.

Peter had to be wrong about a lot of things. I was not using Gary; I was merely moving on. And what's more, I could show Gary how much I liked him. He was steadying me, guiding my way. My right hand slipped out of his and joined my left one behind his neck. His freed hand found a spot lower on my back. I tightened

162

my arms around his neck and, although he seemed a bit surprised, he responded with his own arms.

"Hey," he said later, "this is nice, but I think the music's stopped." He tugged at my arms gently, trying to loosen them.

I lifted my cheek from his shoulder, aware for the first time how scratchy the wool had been on my skin. Looking up, I saw a face I scarcely knew at all. Who had I been expecting to see? I felt myself fracturing into a dozen pieces, none of which were wholly in my control, none of which were me.

"Everybody's looking," he said.

I realized then that I was still clinging to him.

"You're new to this sort of thing," Gary continued, "but I'm not. There are some people over there — chaperons, I think — who look extremely offended."

I lowered my arms and glanced at the chaperons, but they had turned to glower at someone else. "Gary, I'm . . . sorry. I wasn't thinking."

"No need to apologize." He had a confused look on his face. His hands lifted and fell, and lifted again.

We studied each other. I realized it might take months before either of us could even guess what the other was thinking or feeling. And maybe we never would . . .

Rachel appeared at my side as if eager to bolster my spirits, sweep away my doubts. She was flushed from dancing and radiant with the good time she was having. Mark hovered over her protectively. The look he gave her made my heart jump.

"We're dying, aren't you?" she said. "I mean, it must

be a hundred degrees in here. Ah — liquid refreshment. Mark, please could I have some?"

Mark was already on his way to wait on line for two small Dixie cups of punch.

"Having fun, you two?" Rachel grinned slyly at Gary.

"Absolutely," he answered and then seemed to check it out with me.

I nodded and then stared longingly toward the punch. Gary took the hint and joined Mark in line. I waited for Rachel to say something, confident it would be what I needed to hear, some kind of reassurance.

She moved closer. "I saw you slip off with Peter. How'd that go?"

"He was jealous, I guess."

Rachel snorted. "Oh, that makes a heap of sense. Mark saw you too. I told him that he was an old boyfriend. Hope you don't mind. He promised not to mention it to Gary. It's not like you left to neck or something." She paused and then raised her eyebrows at me.

"Of course not," I assured her, a bit stung that she had even wondered. What exactly would Mark tell Gary? Maybe Mark had assumed we'd gone off to "neck or something."

"Rachel —"

"Here you go," Mark said as he handed Rachel her punch. His eyes said that he wanted her to himself again, and he and Rachel left.

Gary brought our punch and started asking me about the courses I was taking this year.

"Oh, the usual stuff." I realized that I was intimidated again by Gary's private-school education. "Nothing like what you're used to. The English classes here are so inadequate — the standard Swift, Melville, pinch of Shakespeare — but I'm thinking about being a writer someday, so I'll take what I can get, I guess." This revelation surprised me. I had barely admitted to myself what I wanted to do.

Gary grinned at me, relieved me of the soggy cup and took my hand. "Maybe you'll find a special teacher or else go ahead and read beyond what they give you. Branch out, you know? One book always leads to others, just like one thought generates lots of ideas. I'll bet you'll be a dynamite writer."

I smiled, glad that I had confided in Gary. My dream was safe, and so, I thought, was I.

The music resumed, and he guided me back to the floor. He made a quick survey of the people around us, seemed satisfied, and then took me tentatively back into his arms.

*

I had always hated the awkwardness at the end of double dates. There is an inevitable lack of privacy, and whether you decide to go ahead and make out or hold back prudishly, you can't win. I was not surprised when it was decided that I would be dropped at home first. Without hesitating even a second, Gary got out of the car, circled around to open my door, and escorted me to the front porch.

"They aren't likely to mind waiting out there for a minute or two," he said just before stooping to kiss me.

"Gary," I whispered, pulling away a few inches. "My dad. I mean, he might be . . . waiting up . . . or something."

"You expect any trouble?"

"Trouble? No, he just . . . well, he usually waits up, is all." This lie, I told myself, is necessary to protect Gary's feelings.

"Okay. Next time I'll have my car. We can" — he kissed me again — "say good-night properly."

"Will there be a next time?" The question just slipped out.

Gary seemed surprised. "Well, of course there will, if I have anything to say about it." He looked up and into the house. I felt the muscles of his arms tense up. "If your father permits it, that is."

"Gary —"

He brushed my cheek and then my forehead with the soft center of his lips. "Next time." And he was gone.

When he opened the car door, the light exposed Rachel and Mark in a tight embrace. They blinked at him and then the door slammed shut. I turned to go inside. The house was dark and inviting. I sighed and closed my eyes, glad to be home, hoping to be left alone. But when I opened my eyes, I saw that Dad had turned on his bedroom light.

"Dad?"

"I'll be right out."

I didn't know how frightened to be. He had said we would "talk later." That didn't sound too bad; in fact, it might accomplish something important. I was reasonably sure that I had not, at least consciously, used Gary to rebel against Dad, as Peter had suspected. But I couldn't deny that things might be working out that way.

I sat down in the living room, in the dark, slipping off my shoes and leaning back to take several deep breaths. "Your dad," Mom would often say to me, "is someone to contend with, but not someone to fear. He loves you so very much."

I didn't ask Mom for any more encouragement than that, or for any advice. Breathing deeply and waiting, I felt Mom's arms — the skin so soft I used to tease her that she had baby skin — touch me lightly and then stand by. I felt her trust in me, and I was adopting it as my own.

"Have a nice time?" Dad's voice startled me. "Mandy?"

"Yes. I had a nice time." I realized, too late, that his question had been sarcastic.

He grunted.

"I suppose you're pretty mad, huh?"

"You're right about that much."

I waited for him to elaborate, still feeling groggy, still feeling Mom's arms nearby.

"Sometimes," he said, and then cleared his throat. "Sometimes I think maybe, without your . . . mother, without her way of making everybody feel okay, we are just plain headed for trouble."

"Dad, it's nothing we can't handle."

"I'm not so sure," he said. "I've been lying here thinking all night about how to deal with this . . . this Gary situation —"

"He's not a situation."

"— and all I've come up with is to ground you. Because"— he stopped me from protesting — "you disobeyed and deceived me. You made a fool of me."

"No, I —"

"I'm too tired to deal with you anymore right now. You're grounded for two weeks." He turned abruptly.

"Two weeks! Wait — you said we'd talk."

He headed back to his room, which still provided the only light in the house. "And" — he hesitated by his door — "of course, you won't be going out with Gary again." His door shut tight behind him.

"Some talk!" I threw my shoes at his door, one missing but the other hitting squarely in the middle. This would surely get him back out here, maybe to face me, the way I wanted to face him. But the door stayed shut, and his last words hung in the air undisturbed.

16

"Y OU'RE WHAT?" Rachel asked Monday night on the phone.

"Grounded for two weeks. Where the heck were you all weekend? I must have tried a hundred times to call you."

"I'm sorry, Mandy. I was at my grandma's in Wisconsin. The whole family was there. Didn't I tell you we were going? Gosh, he was really mad, huh?"

I didn't respond. Rachel's absence had made me feel abandoned again, and I'd thought I was all over that sort of thing.

"I guess you don't want to hear about me and Mark." She tried to laugh me out of my mood. "Can you believe this — *me*, in love?"

"That's nice."

"Mandy, I'm sorry. I guess my being so happy is really lousy timing for you, but I do care, really. Tell me about it. I worried about you all day. Can't you go to school, either?"

"Of course I can. I just chose not to go today. I hardly

left my room, in fact. It nearly drove me out of my mind. Mostly I scratched at some loose paint and tried to think. Then I worried about getting lead poisoning or something, so I tried to write."

"What — a diary?"

"Sort of."

"What'd your dad say about your skipping school?"

"Nothing. I told him I was sick. You haven't heard the worst of it. I can't go out with Gary again, ever. At least that's what Dad says, but I'd like to know how he can control who I go out with once I leave this prison next year."

Rachel sighed. "Well, parents have a way of controlling you even if you're not living with them anymore. You'd better level with Gary, and you'd also better try to patch things up with your dad. Maybe he'll come around. Maybe if you'd told him before, he wouldn't have gotten so mad."

"I know, I know." My head ached with so many *maybes* and so much wondering why.

When I hung up the phone, I felt alone again. Why couldn't I stop needing other people so much?

Dad was outside, much as he had been all day Saturday and Sunday, sometimes working, mostly just wandering around his fields. He seemed to be looking for solace there, or perhaps company. Maybe he talked to plants, hugged the earth or whatever — I didn't know for sure. But it seemed to me that he cared more about the farm than he did about me.

Dad and I had spoken less than a dozen words between us in the last three days. In my mind I explained to perfection why I had done what I had done and he admitted he had overreacted, said that Gary seemed like a nice young man and let's just forget all this fussing. But all those words remained caught inside me as though they were upside-down and on end, sharp corners sticking out to remind me of their presence.

Monday-night television saved the evening. Dad and I shared the room, looked in the same direction and even laughed at the same times, but we carried our hurt and weariness to our beds at 10:00 sharp and then let darkness and night-stillness try to fill up the empty spaces we had made of our house.

In the middle of the night I thought I heard him in my brothers' old room, then rambling through other parts of the house. I remembered what he had said once about how empty the rooms had become for him. I was beginning to understand what he'd meant except that *my* empty rooms were not a part of this structure we called our home, but rather inside me.

People who had occupied some of my rooms seemed to be vacating them lately. Peter, my dad, Lynn. And, of course, Mom, although her room, her place inside me, felt wonderfully and conveniently open to her. I knew that it would always remain so. I also knew there were plenty of other people around who could be good occupants, but maybe they wouldn't be permanent, or fill every corner.

*

The next morning I went to school and plowed through the barrier each day had become. First hour, second hour, third hour, lunch, fourth, fifth, sixth and seventh hours, home on the bus, homework, dinner, television, bed. Sleep allowed me to coast pleasantly from the last day, smack up against the next. And it all began again. No movies, nothing after school, no dates (as if I were being flooded with invitations anyway). But the two weeks would pass eventually.

Gary called a few days after Homecoming and I told him, as matter-of-factly as possible, that I wouldn't be able to go out with him again, at least for a while. Instead of the outrage I had expected from him, I heard a humble "I see. I understand."

"Maybe later. I'll work on him."

"Call me if things change," he said before hanging up.

It was then that I heard in his voice what was happening inside him. It was quiet but frustrated resignation. He'd had plenty of practice with it before. For all I knew, he had been expecting my dad to keep me away from him, just like this, as if he were infected with something horrible, as if he might infect me.

I see. I understand. Call me if things change. His words kept me awake for several nights. What must it feel like to have parents keep their children away from you? And then not even to be able to lash back. To accept things as they are, at least for now. "Call me if things change." As if "things" would ever change.

Chalk up another one for *them*, he might be saying. The score was probably still weighted against him, but by the time he graduated from an Ivy League college and took his wool suits and perfect manners to some progressive city to teach, the tally would be heavily in his favor. My chalk mark would have gotten lost in his dusty past. My name would probably elude him, but I guessed that the expression on my father's face that night would not.

I filled much of my time writing down my thoughts and feelings about all that had been happening. Words on paper, blue ink in a school notebook, would stay put for me to examine with a cool eye, even to modify.

I spent one evening listing things about myself I didn't like and then crossing each one out. Somewhat giddy after that, I then scrawled in a huge, forceful hand descriptions of the better me and then mentally penetrated the words themselves, letting them adapt to me. I crawled in and out of all the *o*'s in *good-looking* (discarding *beautiful* as too fancy), and slid up and down the letters in *kind* and *intelligent*. I performed graceful looping acrobatics at the beginning of *feminine*, but then tumbled off at the end of the word. What on earth did it mean to be feminine, anyway? Warm and sexy? Soft and submissive? I ended up leaving an ornate trio of question marks after that word, followed by a few swaggering, potent exclamation points.

My new journal gave me scribbly reassurance that I could write, as well as an uncritical "listener." But other times a white page in a notebook seemed a sterile, unreceptive place for my confidences. So I would spend hours on the phone with Rachel. We talked about everything from the approaching wintry air and the possibility of skiing together soon to some books we were both reading. I found myself compulsively thanking her. "For what?" she asked for a while, but when I could never answer, she simply said "You're welcome."

*

One day soon after I was no longer grounded, I got off the bus to find Peter's car parked by our house. Relief was, surprisingly, my strongest reaction to seeing it there.

He was alone, waiting for me on the front porch. "Hi," he said. "How ya doing?" He sat leaning forward in the love seat, elbows on his knees, fidgety hands dangling.

I sat on the other side of the porch from him, carefully reminding myself that we were mad at each other. I shivered.

"Why don't we go inside?" he asked.

I shook my head. Moving both of us into the house seemed too monumental a task at the moment. "I guess you know I was grounded for two weeks."

He shook his head and then nodded, so I wasn't sure what his answer was. "Been pretty rough? With your dad, I mean?"

"Well, it hasn't been great."

He nodded again. "Don't be too hard on him, Mandy. He's been going through so much lately, he can hardly think straight, I suspect. You really threw him a curve."

"What do you mean?"

"Don't get all defensive again. I didn't mean anything."

Why was I sounding so much angrier than I felt? I

174

wondered. It was probably the same for him. I surprised us both by smiling almost warmly. What I saw when I looked over at him was simply Peter, not Peter-and-Lynn-hurting-Mandy anymore. And not Peter-my-protector, either.

"I suppose," he said uncertainly, "it's absolutely necessary for you to sit all the way over there." He patted his hand on the seat cushion next to him, and I watched the movement from my distance. Nothing dangerous or even especially meaningful there, but still I stayed where I was.

"You look like you could use a hug."

I figured I should be rigid and say "No, thank you." But instead I found myself next to him and his arms pressed around me. I fit my cheek into the almost-soft spot between his shoulder and chest. The muffled beat of his heart brought to mind the trick of putting a ticking clock in a new pup's bed to quiet him.

"Let's not talk," I said, "at least not right now."

I felt his head nod in agreement above mine.

We watched the outside begin to turn dusky and felt the chill that was entering the air but not having much effect on us, huddled together like that. My eyes had been closed for some time when I felt his fingers under my chin. I opened my eyes, and we watched each other for a moment. I saw surprise in his face and wondered if it was the same as I was feeling — surprise at the lack of any strong desire to kiss.

"Not the same, is it?"

I was glad he had been the one to say it, not me. "No, it's not the same."

"I suppose, then . . . that there's really nothing left between us."

"Are you kidding? There's plenty left."

He nodded, and we returned to keeping each other warm.

"But," he began and lifted his head from mine again. "But . . ."

"But what?"

"Never mind. I don't want to spoil this moment by talking too much."

"Oh, go ahead," I said. "That's never stopped you before."

He laughed and held me tighter. "I was just wondering what, exactly, there is between us, then. I hate to be nosy, but . . . well, Lynn would probably like to know. Among others."

"Do you love Lynn?" I asked.

"Me? No, not really. But she's never been able to take care of herself — you know that. She needed somebody, and I needed to be needed. Maybe I still do."

"But, Peter, you and she are lovers, aren't you?"

"No, that's all over. I thought she was what I wanted after you . . . after we broke up. And it was very easy, I guess, to go ahead and, well, you know. But we both knew right away that it wasn't going to work out. To be honest, she's tired of me already. I'm not nearly as exciting as she thought I was."

My first impulse was to toss back a clever "I could've told her that," but I reconsidered. "Then, she was wrong," I said instead. "That's her loss."

176

He didn't reply, but I felt his heartbeat speed up slightly. I found myself anticipating the next beat, and the next, steadying myself with it the way I had so often with Mom's. Then I realized it was my own I was tuned into most of all. It was steady and sure, on its own.

"Mandy?"

"Hm-m-m?"

"Still no kiss, though?"

I sighed and searched for a response. It was true that I wasn't exactly feeling the old tingle, but I was feeling something better, at least for the moment. "Peter, couldn't we . . . uh, maybe work on our friendship for a while? After all, that's more valuable, isn't it?"

"Oh, you're right. Absolutely."

I could tell he wasn't convinced. In fact, I wasn't all that certain about myself — I missed the tingle. But I held firm, reminding myself with a few deep breaths about what was important now. As "just" friends, I was sure we could keep growing, both of us.

"Want to come inside," I asked, "and help me make dinner?"

Peter didn't take time to think about it. "Why not? I'd love to."

17 ⌇

I WAS PLEASED with myself about that dinner, having finally gotten the hang of planning ahead. Well stocked with groceries and clean, the kitchen no longer seemed a setting for struggle and ultimate failure.

After Peter had left and I had turned the oven down to warm, I began to worry about Dad; it was unlike him to come in after dark.

Winter's approach shortened the days in quick bites now, barely noticeable to all but the practiced eye of a farmer. Even though long nights and deadening cold had never seemed to bother Dad before, I wondered if this winter would be different. The longer hours of darkness lengthened the shadows in our mostly empty house. Dad's dread of empty rooms was probably keeping him outside as much as possible.

When I thought I heard the pickup truck approach from a distant field, I sprang into action. Running through all the rooms of the house, I turned on lights so the windows would shine out their welcome.

Lastly, I clicked on the yard-light and then ran out to join Dad, to meet him halfway.

But he jumped down from the cab of his truck and veered into the packing shed.

"Dad?" I followed him into the shed and turned on its yellow overhead light. Lugs of vegetables — mostly late, imperfect ones — still pressed together, their square cardboard forms shoulder-to-shoulder. "Aren't you coming in now?" I asked him.

"What for?" He inspected a few lugs of overripe and cracked tomatoes — canners — and hoisted them all to the door. To sell? I wondered. Or should I have been doing the canning as Mom had always done? Even having assisted her for years, I doubted I would know where to start. There were so many of her chores that I had seemed to deliberately avoid learning, as if that would keep her around longer to do them for me.

"Well, dinner's ready," I said.

"I don't care about that."

"You don't?" If I'd needed a pat on the back for preparing dinner, my own would have had to do.

"Of course not. Somehow food used to seem more important . . . before . . ."

He was restless, and the yellow glare gave him an eerie, haunted look.

"Well, we have to eat."

"Mandy, forget it. All this talk about food sounds just like . . . well, like your mother. Other people miss a meal now and then. They survive."

"I'm sorry, Dad. I was just trying to be more dependable again, like you've been wanting me to be."

179

"Maybe I did for a while, but . . ."

"But I failed miserably?" I laughed softly, and Dad took the cue to do the same.

"No, I was going to say that I finally realized that I wasn't the only one around here with needs."

"I never minded being needed, Dad. It's being . . . oh, I don't know, *possessed* . . . that's what I can't stand anymore."

Dad nodded, but still we avoided each other's eyes. He sat down on an old wooden chair — the sole survivor of his parents' kitchen set. It fretted under his weight.

"It's this farm." He motioned toward the tomatoes near him to represent something much bigger, much more unmanageable. "That's why I need you," Dad continued. "Because of the farm."

I sighed. "I know. You wanted me to marry a farmer and stay here with you."

Dad's head snapped up and he stared at me, squinting in the light. "Is that what you thought I wanted?"

"That's what you told me."

He shook his head.

"Dad, you *did* say that. That talk we had. You know, the day before the Homecoming dance."

"I was just telling you about an old pipe dream of mine. I didn't mean anything serious by it."

"Well, what were you saying, then? What did you want from me?"

"Your advice."

"My what?" I sat down unsteadily on an overturned crate. "You wanted my advice?"

180

"Well, the farm's been weighing heavy on me. I don't know if I should stay here alone, or sell out, or sell part of it, or maybe lease some land. I've never been . . . so confused."

He picked up a grotesquely large canning tomato, and with the fingertips of his other hand, he traced the black crevices radiating from its stem. Raising it to his mouth to take a bite out of it, he settled its shining surface against his chin instead.

"Dad, why didn't you ask me, then? I would have been so glad to talk it all over with you."

"I thought I should" — he took a small bite and chewed thoughtfully — "but then I realized that I'd be putting you in that spot again, depending on you as if you didn't . . . well, have a life of your own to plan out."

How long, I wondered, had we been keeping things from each other for the sake of independence? Maybe some sort of *inter*dependence was what we should be after.

"I can't believe this," I said. "It's like we haven't been speaking the same language, or maybe there's been too much distracting us, I don't know. But I was so mad at you. That's why I couldn't tell you about Gary. I knew you'd disapprove, but I couldn't stand having to be your little girl anymore, always going after your approval, Peter's approval, everybody's but my own."

"Well, now." Dad cleared his throat. "Since you brought him up . . ."

"Peter?"

181

"No." He gave me a look that said *you know who I mean.*

"Dad, you're so wrong about Gary."

"I know that you think I'm wrong, but I . . . I still can't let you date him. I've thought about it more than you can imagine. People my age were just plain brought up differently. It's hard to change all of a sudden. I'll bet *his* parents feel exactly the same way."

"But things really are changing, Dad, with or without you."

"Are you so sure that there ever will be a day when a child of mixed blood will feel like he completely belongs, somewhere?"

"What does a 'child of mixed blood' have to do with anything?" I had to put off his question until I could give it some thought. "Gary's a really nice guy. That's all."

"I'm sure he is and that's what scares me most. You'll fall for him for sure. It'll be a mess."

"Dad, why do you insist on thinking marriage and children? I just want to get to know him. He's worth . . . he's —"

"He's worth what? The risk?"

"Okay. I guess I was going to say that. But since when are you against taking risks?"

"Since . . . just lately, I guess."

"Oh, Dad. . . ." I gave up arguing with him — we would always disagree on certain things. It didn't really matter. What I wanted now was to reconcile.

"Dad, if you still think my advice might help . . ."

He returned the tomato to its place, minus an almost invisible bite, and nodded.

"Well, I can't imagine you leaving here. You love this place. What else would you do? What other kind of job?"

He smiled wryly as he stared at his bulky, beat-up hands. The tip of one finger was missing and had been for as long as I could remember. "Well," he said, "I was considering brain surgery."

It was so good to hear him joke like he used to. I said, "They'd never find rubber gloves to get past your knuckles."

An image, so quick I almost missed it, presented itself to me: Mom massaging and working perfumed lotion into the deep creases of Dad's hands, so tenderly, somehow getting around his resistance to pampering. I tried to retrieve the image, to sharpen it, define Mom's profile as she bent over Dad's fingers. But, on second thought, I pushed it carefully aside.

"This farm," I began again, "this place is only forty-some acres. It's never been too much for you before, and it won't be now, either. Hire a couple of kids next summer. And," I added, with a barely concealed sigh, "I'll be here, of course."

"No. No, it's time you got a regular summer job. Get out from under. Your mother" — Dad swallowed hard —"used to say that."

A heaviness in my chest lifted. "Do you mean it?" I asked.

"Yes," he said, drawing the word out.

"Thanks, Dad. I'd like that a lot." I felt my face stretch into a smile.

"As far as the house goes . . ." Dad's voice was wavery.

"Oh, the house. Well, I don't think it will seem so empty, even next year when I leave, once you get used to it. Besides, you'll have us kids visiting regularly . . . and grandkids — that's right! More than you can handle. You'll see." I got up and looked out the door at the brightly lit house.

Dad stood and stretched, elbows pointing at nine and three o'clock. A loose button sprang from his shirt, and we watched it roll and then spiral to a stop. We both leaned to pick it up at the same time, and then looked at each other a little shyly.

When I started to hug Dad tentatively, he responded with a bear hug that took my breath away. But it was easy to breathe again afterward. Maybe easier than it had been for a long time.